The Masquerade

V.M. Jackson

The Masquerade

Copyright © 2019

THE MASQUERADE is a work of fiction. The events and characters that are described are imaginary and are not intended to refer to specific places or living persons.

Chapter 1

Mannequin

"*Yes, I can switch you with my 2:30. I'm sure that'll give you enough time to catch your flight.. that's fine... Great. I'll see you then, Pam. Mhm. Bye,*" Quinn hung up her cellphone and glanced over at the clock. "Oh, Jesus, it's almost ten am." Scrambling out of bed, she tossed her satin cream sheets off of her body.

"So much for *breakfast,*" Andre sounded annoyed as he stood in the bathroom adjusting his tie in the mirror. Quinn paused in the midst of her scrambling and peered into the bathroom at her husband.

"You know what," she raised an eyebrow, "you've been admiring yourself in the mirror for the past thirty-five minutes, but you couldn't remind me of the time?"

"And you've done a great job of *timing* me in the bathroom but couldn't keep track of a more important time frame...like having breakfast with your husband," he declared, unbothered by her attitude. He smiled at himself in the mirror before spinning around to face Quinn in all his grandeur. "Anyway, how do I look?" He gave her a full view of his tailored black suit, and charming red tie.

"You look like someone I once knew," Quinn gave her husband a soft once over, gazing into his eyes. "He was the most beautiful man on the face of the earth, inside *and* out. He asked me to marry him almost a decade ago, and he always treated me like I was the wind beneath his wings. But for the last 6 months, he's treated me more like the gum beneath his shoe," her stare turned to ice as she shook her head and hurried past the bathroom into her walk-in closet. Quinn's words were an echo Andre's ego certainly didn't want to hear this morning. Watching her walk away, he rubbed a hand down his neck, quietly retracting all the bad things he'd said to her lately. He knew his marriage was in trouble, and he knew *he* was the cause of it. Despite his black heart over the last six months, Pastor Andre Bentley was still an *Adonis* amongst men. He was charming, smart, smooth, and tailored by success.

He carried his six-foot-four stature with easy self-assurance, and the *deepest* hickory brown eyes, rich as the earth's soil. His prominent jaw curved gracefully around the strength of his neck. He had strong arms, bold legs, and a firm chest, all dipped in melted, Belgian truffle. One look had women swooning at the sight of him. Just a word from his lips had even the gayest of women flushing shades of red. Andre had the heart of a lion and the soul of an angel. His congregation *loved* him. They were drawn to him; they clung to his every word and could reciprocate his smile so quickly. Everyone wanted to be close to him. Pastor Bentley was a powerful, anointed man of God who went above and beyond for his ministry. He selflessly gave back to the community and treated his members like they were his own family.

"I'm sorry you feel that way," Andre muttered, "and I'm also sorry we don't have time to talk about how you feel."

"Right, because there aren't enough hours in the day to fix what's wrong with me- what's wrong with *us,*" Quinn shuffled angrily through her skirt suits.

Andre walked out of the bathroom. "Listen, it's been a long morning for me. I was up until midnight talking to Dawn about the church finances, and then Deacon Greg called me about the balcony. Apparently, the whole upstairs is flooded from the rain. And Bishop Warren called me about speaking at his men's conference. I didn't get to my sermon until about four in the morning, and I've been up ever since." He walked over to Quinn, securing his arms around her waist, and buried his face in her neck. "But in lieu of my busy schedule and lack of sleep, I was looking forward to having breakfast with you. We do need to talk. *I did try.*"

"I'm sorry," Quinn tilted her head onto her husband's shoulder, tired of arguing. *She missed them being this close.* "I got caught up, too. Wendy woke me up at five am about one of her daughters. You remember Hanna don't you?"

"I do," he replied, "the one I baptized last year. She won the scholarship from the college ministry for her good grades."

"Exactly, but that was t*hen*. She went off to college and went *ballistic.* That girl is not the same person you put under water," Quinn shook her head. "She's turned gothic and she's experimenting with drugs and tattoos. It's horrible."

"What?" he winced.

Quinn nodded, "Yeah, and now Wendy is going ballistic right along with her. Hanna came home last night, completely high off a bunch of street drugs, so Wendy tied her up and locked her in the basement.

She wouldn't let her out until she talked to a professional."

"So she called *you*," Andre chuckled.

"She called *me*…" Quinn sighed, "I was on the phone with her for hours."

"Well, you're the psychologist."

Quinn glanced at the clock, making a mental note of the passing time. She broke away from her husband, grabbing a navy blue skirt suit from her closet. After laying it on their bed, she removed her oversized nightgown, exposing her almond colored frame. Pulling out her scrunchie, heaps of molten, bronzed gold tumbled out of her scalp and cascaded down her back like a waterfall…*Andre watched in awe.* Despite their rocky relationship, he was still drawn to her beauty.

Quinn was five-foot-five, one hundred and forty pounds of pure, Amazonian woman. She had a hazelnut complexion, and a coke bottle figure that was so toned and graceful, it looked airbrushed. She had cherry lips, and white teeth; *she was a beautiful sight to behold.* Her eyes, well for a lack of a better word, were gray; but that one-word description wouldn't do them justice. They were like smoke; gray and full of heat. They glistened brightly, yet they were very pale. They were cold, like a slab of ice. They were the type of gray that sparkled like diamonds, or the color of ash remnants after a roaring fire. *They were winter gray.* Quinn was so breathtakingly beautiful, she was almost too seamless to be real; much like a *mannequin*. She had a gentle spirit that made being around her relaxing. Her inner beauty was more striking than her outward appearance. When she smiled and laughed, you couldn't help but smile along with her. To be in her company was to feel that you too, were someone.

If the Gods were real, Quinn would've certainly been their masterpiece.

"I am a psychologist Monday through Friday, from eight am until six pm. *Not* five in the morning. Plus, she's not my client. Wendy is my friend and a member of our church. The psychologist in me told me not to even answer my phone because I knew it was drama, but the First Lady in me felt like I had no choice. *It's not easy being married to a pastor."*

"You think my job as the *Pastor* is any easier?" Andre caught wind of her derision.

"I didn't mean it like that," Quinn lowered her brow.

"I beg to differ," Andre grew annoyed. "This is the third time this week you've mentioned it," he fussed, "like *my* position has such a stressful effect on *you*."

"Let's just drop it, Andre. I can see where this is going," Quinn walked into the bathroom and turned on the shower.

"Then keep your *smart* comments to yourself."

"Yup," Quinn disappeared into the shower, letting out a sigh. The hot water ran over her curls, drenching and straightening them immediately. She had so much to say to him but decided it would be safer to keep her thoughts to herself.

Andre and Quinn met at ten years old in a hair salon, while their mothers got their hair done. While their parent's first introduction formed an immediate friendship, Quinn and Andre couldn't stand the sight of one another. They hated being forced on play dates and having to pretend to get along, but as long as their parents remained friends, they had no choice in the matter. Andre constantly teased Quinn about her exotic eye color, comparing her to an alien from outer space, and Quinn thought Andre was the most annoying little boy in all of Virginia. As the years went by, it seemed they'd *never* get along. That is, until they turned thirteen and Quinn was asked to the Valentine's Day dance by Joseph, the male heartthrob of Barry Farms middle school. The second Andre found out, he walked through the school with a vengeance, looking for Joseph. When he found him, Joseph was in the gym behind the bleachers with Quinn, intending to kiss her. Jealousy filled Andre's heart causing him to hit Joseph so hard, he knocked him out cold. Quinn's mouth dropped open. She wanted to scream, but before she could, Andre grabbed her and gave her the kind of kiss that made her forget her name. They've been together ever since. Over the last twenty years, they finished middle school, high school, and college together. They were married three years after undergrad and were just a few months into their ninth year of marriage. Andre grew up in a very spiritual home. He was the son of the late Phillip and Guilda Bentley. He served as a deacon, armor bearer, and assistant pastor to his father until five years ago when his father and mother were killed in a plane crash. Since then, he and Quinn have taken over his parents Megachurch in Virginia. Quinn went straight from her undergraduate studies to pursue a dual degree in Psychology. To date, she's owned her own practice for seven years and has become one of Richmond's most popular Psychologists. Quinn and Andre were the epitome of love growing up. They were the kind of couple everyone aspired to mimic, and had the type of love that brought peace, harmony, and hope to everyone that knew them. Quinn was Andre's weakness. She was the medicine to his mind, body, *and* soul. No one could ever love her the way he did. He protected her with his life and had the utmost respect for her. Her love was like opening a book and reading a language he'd never seen before. She was the trap he'd been waiting to fall into his entire life. Andre believed that true love, loved in kind deeds, thoughtful actions, truthfulness, and trustworthiness. He expressed all of that to Quinn and never grew tired. *Until six months ago.*

"Anyhow, I have a christening to attend later on, and a baby shower on Saturday," he continued his heartless rant, "I expect you'll be alongside me?"

"No, I can't. Sorry," she answered, "I have work and meetings until six, and then I have dinner plans with my friends."

"Quinn, you're my wife," his jaw tightened at her nonchalant tone, "it'd be nice if you could act like it from time to time and *show up* to these kinds of events."

"You know what else would be nice, Andre? If you'd take a break from christening babies and attending baby showers, and make a baby with your *own* wife."

"Really?" He bellowed, baring his teeth. Swinging open the glass shower door, he cut the water off. Quinn gasped as the cold air from the bathroom slapped her naked body.

"Does that make you feel better?" She replied. Quinn grabbed the shower door back from him and slammed it shut. Forcefully, Andre gripped the outside shower handle once more and violently swung it open sending Quinn shuffling out of the shower as she held on to the inside handle.

"I'm so sick of your *shit*," he shouted.

"Oh, I'm sorry, *Pastor,*" Quinn shot back.

"Okay..." he pointed his index finger in her face, "keep it up."

"You know what, I will keep it up." She snatched her towel from the floor and wrapped it around herself. "I'm sick of this charade I'm forced to play as if everything is alright with us when it's not, and you know it's not. I don't know what I did to you, or what you did to yourself," she sneered, giving him a disgusted once over, "but you've become mean, nasty, and extremely rude to me."

"Oh Gosh," he flung his arms in the air, storming out of the bathroom.

"No," she rushed behind him, "stop walking away and *listen* to me."

"I don't have time," Andre snatched his coat from the closet and grabbed his cellphone out of his pocket. Quinn snatched his coat out of one hand and slapped his cellphone from the other hand so hard, it flew across the room and shattered against the wall.

"Listen to me!" She screamed. Andre's eyes widened at her temper. Normally, Quinn was meek as a kitten, but not today. The kitten was out of town; only the sleeping tiger was home. *And he just woke it up.*

I'm not gonna let you continue to treat me like this. This isn't right, nor is it *fair*," she fussed, "I'm a good wife! I'm a good person! You need to walk out of this house and go find the man I married," she glared at Andre. He stared back with hard eyes that never blinked. His heartless gaze bought tears to her eyes. *She couldn't believe him.* "What is happening to you?" She put her hand on his cheek and moved in to find the answer in his eyes. Andre wanted to respond. He had so much to say to her. He wanted to apologize to her, to hold her, to kiss her, to rush into her arms and cry, to tell her the truth. His heart wanted to speak to the woman he loved, but his demons spoke first.

"Don't touch me," moving back, he slapped her hand away. "We'll finish this discussion another day. I have to get to my church. You know, the one you're too *busy* to attend."

"Andre, I am not some discussion that can be saved for another day," her voice shook as tears trailed her eyes, "I am your wife."

"That's the problem. Maybe you aren't fit to be *my* wife anymore!" He burst into flames. Quinn froze. The shock registered on her face before it even reached her brain. Andre grabbed his coat from the floor and stormed out of the room. "I'll be at Sprint getting a *new phone*," he shook his head. "The church meeting to discuss the building expansion project is at six o'clock, if you care to be there. If not, *whatever.* Have a good day." The front door slammed shut, in sync with the insults that slammed into Quinn's chest. Sliding lifelessly down her bedroom wall, she began to cry. Her heartache was like a wolf eating at her chest, tearing its way to her trembling heart. It threatened to devour her, eat her whole, and leave nothing but scraps behind. Quinn was done. Done in, over-done, and undone. *She was looking for the place hearts went to resign.*

Chapter 2

Pandora

Jackson pinned his fiancée, Pandora, against the full-sized window of her secluded high-rise office on the thirty-fifth floor. She moaned softly, sealing her eyes shut as he kissed her neck and took in the aroma of her Chanel perfume.

"It's been a while," he spoke in between kisses, "I've missed you so much."

"I've missed you too," she replied.

"Prove it."

"Later," she grinned, opening her eyes as she bought their lustful greeting back to reality. "I have a lot of work to do today."

"Surely you have a lunch break soon," he leaned in to kiss her again.

"Soon? It's eight o'clock in the morning," Pandora giggled, accepting his intoxicating kiss just as her secretary's voice emerged through the personal PA system in her office.

"Anna, you have Grace on line one, and Jessie wants to know your decision about the partner referral ASAP."

"Tell Jessie to take her partner referral, and shove it up her behind. I'll take line one, thanks honey." Moving around Jackson, she glided around her desk like a slinking panther, in search of her phone.

"You know, for the longest time, I always wondered how you got the nickname "Pandora," Jackson chuckled. "When I first met you I found it hard to believe your personality reminded people of a Greek goddess who unleashed all hell over humanity. At first glance, you just appear to be this drop-dead gorgeous attorney, and-"

"My sentiments *exactly*," Pandora interrupted with a smirk, "because something so pretty wouldn't hurt a fly, right?" she rubbed her hands together in that classic way that villains do.

"Of course it wouldn't," Jackson shook his head, amused.

"Good morning, Grace," Jackson watched Pandora answer her phone, quickly adjusting her tone into a more innocent one. He was always amazed at her ability to chameleonize herself when needed. Every time he stepped into her presence, he was impressed. Joanna Wilson was like a magazine cut out, dropped onto the Virginia sidewalk. She stood five-foot-four, one hundred and twenty pounds. She had skin the color of a soft harvest moon, mysterious, amber colored eyes, and a confident, sexy strut that told the world I'm *beautiful*. Her shoulder length hair reminded Jackson of the rich soil of the valleys after spring rains, almost black in the shadows. When she stepped into the light, it was a rich brown, almost with an undertone of red beneath. With a delightfully innocent smile and two deep hollow dimples, she was easily the most beautiful woman that Jackson had ever seen. Indeed, she was a sight to behold, *but a dangerous one*. Pandora served as one of the top defense attorneys in the country. Many times, criminals contacted her with the most unbelievable crimes. Pandora mopped up their disasters, defended their innocence, and was paid handsomely to do so. In the eight years she's worked for her firm, she'd only lost one case, and currently held the record for the most civil cases won by any attorney. Jackson surveyed her office. It was ostentatious, reassuringly expensive, and in the most exclusive part of the city. His fiancée had perfected the art of argument in legalistic language and demanded an exorbitant fee. She drove an exotic car and had an executive condo with so much square footage, she needed several maids to clean it. Pandora was a wolf among sheep. She was cut-throat, and *definitely* not one to play with. She had an easygoing style, but it was her conniving persona that made her dangerous. She hid behind her beauty and could disarm any opponent with one flash of her dimples. Though a very good friend and great business partner, when pushed, her temper could clear a football stadium. Her tantrums were *legendary*. At its peak, the whole world could hear it. Pandora was smart, cunning, and sharp as a tack. Everywhere she went, her persona attracted more men than she knew what to with, but she never paid them any mind. She'd dated and fell in love once upon a time, but that fairytale had long ended. Like any female, she hoped to settle down and start a family someday, but after law school and her career, love and marriage were the last thing on her mind. That is until she crossed paths with Jackson. They met four years ago while Pandora cross-examined one of her witnesses during a case. Forced into random Jury Duty, Jackson sat in the jury, watching Pandora like a hawk. Her form fitting black pantsuit fit her body like a glove. Her black pumps clicked loudly on the courtroom floor as she paced back and forth like a catwalk model. In her ordinariness, Jackson thought she was stunning. Something radiated from within that rendered her irresistible, and he had to have her. As Pandora turned to face the Jury, she stumbled on her words, noticing Jackson peering at her with his hazel eyes. His facial features were very boyish; big eyes, soft skin, and a button nose. There was nothing rugged about him at all; even his face was smooth shaven. He had waist length dreadlocks, and a charming smile. Pandora had always gone for men with a more dangerous look, but Jackson slayed her with how kind he looked, *how safe*. After being flustered by his presence, Pandora struggled to finish her piece and sat down in her seat. The sexual tension radiating between Jackson and Pandora filled the courtroom. There was something about him, and whatever it was, it was doing something to her. The minute court was over, Pandora rushed out of the courtroom and high tailed it to the private family bathroom to fix her flustered demeanor. She walked into the bathroom, closed the door and spun around with her body pressed against the doorframe. Letting out a sigh, she closed her eyes, envisioning the way Jackson undressed her with his eyes.

"Thinking about me?" A deep baritone voice filled the restroom. Pandora's eyes popped open just in time to see Jackson's six-foot-six frame standing in front of her. They stared deeply at each other as Jackson's muscles tensed and Pandora's heart raced. The lust within the small family bathroom came crashing to a halt as Jackson quickly moved into Pandora, and they kissed wildly. That one time was all it took. *Pandora was hooked like an addict.*

Jackson was an accountant who spent the majority of his time traveling the country in search of new clients. However, every time he paid Virginia a visit, he made sure to stop by and open Pandora's box. Jackson fulfilled all of her forbidden sexual fantasies and took her on an endless romantic rollercoaster. Pandora was so sprung, even *she* didn't understand her behavior. She had a lot of respect for her body and had never just given it away so loosely. In the past, a man needed at least 5 references and 3 letters of recommendation before she even considered giving out her phone number. Maybe it was loneliness. Maybe the volume of her career had been turned up so loud, she couldn't hear her heart begging for attention; begging for something real...Whatever it was, it caused her to fall head over heels for Jackson. Three years later, their sexual relationship turned into something much deeper and they began to date. Suddenly, their lack of consistent communication began to bother Pandora. Their sexual relationship was fun at the spontaneous level, but now that love was involved, she didn't approve of it at all. Jackson traveled throughout the country every week for different clients, and Pandora couldn't keep up with him. Sometimes, it'd be months before he could circle back to Virginia, and when he did he could only stay for a weekend. With her demanding job and him traveling to different time zones, they could barely keep up a phone or text conversation. Still, like any fool in love, she said, *"yes"* nine months ago, when he asked her to marry him.

Jackson walked closer to her, erasing the remaining distance between them. He used both of his big hands to glide up her thighs.

"Stop, Jackson," she flagged him away, moving the phone from one ear to the other. He paid her no mind.

"Has your husband locked you out of all the accounts?" She asked, attempting to focus on her client. "No. *No*. Do not contact him, and certainly do not harass him via text, or on social networks, he will use it against you in court." Jackson began kissing her neck. "Jackson," she nudged him away, annoyed. "I really mean it, *stop it*." Jackson grinned at her disheveled demeanor, continuing to push the envelope. Five minutes later, he'd interrupted her with kisses, and sent her mind off focus so much, Pandora replied to her client with, "Grace, I'll call you back," she forced the words out of her mouth before forcibly ending the call. "Are you serious?" She looked up at him, flustered and annoyed.

"I just want some attention, that's all," he nuzzled his face into her neck, "I haven't seen you all month."

"And whose fault is that? You went missing for 30 days and refused to contact me," she pushed him aside and moved to a safer distance. "Now that you're back, you think you can just barge into my office and seduce me out of my workday?"

"I think I can do what I want. You're my fiancée," he smirked.

"Oh, we're engaged again?" Pandora asked sarcastically.

"We've been engaged. You know that."

"But I'm not your wife."

"*Yet.*"

"Well...when, Jackson," she turned to face him.

"When the time is right, sweetheart. I have a lot going on at work. It's hard for me to stay in one spot."

Pandora walked over to her mirror to fix her hair. "I don't get you. We've been engaged for the last nine months, which is fine by me. I was never in a rush.

I don't have to be married, this was *your* idea. You proposed to me and told me to start planning immediately. You got me excited about love, and the idea of what could be, but every time I create the date and move forward, you come up with a new excuse," she shook her head. "You disappear for *weeks*, I don't see you, I don't hear from you… then you pop up in my office as if everything is fine and dandy."

"Well," he smirked, "is it?"

"No," Pandora spun back around to face him with her arms folded across her chest, "*hell* no it isn't. Are you serious?"

"Anna, I have clients and work. I can't slow down from my career to stroke your insecurities," he replied, "you of all people should understand that."

"Excuse me?" Pandora proclaimed angrily, moving toward him with protruding eyes.

"Wait, don't get upset," he rebutted quickly with outstretched arms. "What I'm saying is, I apologize for continuously stringing you along. How about we just live in the moment and forget the last nine months?"

"How about you get out of my office before I have security drag you out?" Pandora's defensive side rose to the occasion.

"Come on, don't do that to me. I love you. Now, how about that early lunch break?" He smirked.

Pandora briefly glared at him before walking over to her desk to reach for the security button.

"Stop it," grabbing her arm, Jackson pulled her close.

"Let go of me," Pandora struggled against his grip.

"Marry me," he blurted, "next month."

Pandora stopped her struggle and peered up at him. She quickly re-tracked her memory, remembering all the other times he'd lied to her. She wasn't about to look like a fool again. "Jackson, stop it- I'm serious, just stop it," she pushed him away. Her bruised ego couldn't take being strung along any longer.

"I'm serious this time," he pulled her back with a glare that demanded to be taken seriously. "I'm sorry, Anna, I do love you. I want to marry you, but I'm afraid. Okay? *There…*"

"Afraid?" She furrowed.

"Yes, I'm afraid," he flung his arms into the air as if finally releasing the truth he'd held on to for so long. "Everything I've ever committed myself to, I've lost. From jobs to good women, I always seem to screw it up. And then I found you and began to live a life free of titles, and rules. Together we just did whatever we felt like doing, in whatever moment that presented itself. You didn't pressure me about being in a relationship or talk my head off about marriage. And I fell in love with you. I fell in love with your smile," he caressed her face, "those dimples, and your personality. You're so powerful, yet so *gentle*. Being around you has breathed so much life into me. You've been my medicine in more ways than you'll know. I don't want to lose that."

"Jackson," her soft eyes lifted to meet his, "we don't have to get married if you don't want to. I love you, but I'm content with the way things are. If a title is going to change the way you love me, then I don't want it."

"But, I want it. I want *you*. It feels right, you and I. I want you forever, and its time for me to stop running from love." He let out a deep breath. "Please, let's set a date…*Let's make this happen.* I have a business trip to Puerto Rico next month. You've been dying to go there. Let's have a destination wedding. Just you and I, or whomever you want to bring. I don't care as long as you're there."

"You're really serious?" A slow building smile spread across her face.

"Yes, Anna, I am," he leaned in and kissed her just as her secretary's voice emerged through the PA system a second time.

"Anna, Dr. Winston is here for his appointment."

"Buzz him in, and send him up," snapping out of their moment, Pandora walked over to her desk.

"Listen, I have a meeting with a client, like right now. Can we finish this later?"

"Of course. I have an 8 pm flight to Dallas, tonight. I'm gonna head back to my hotel and grab some shut-eye. Call me when you're available," Jackson reached down and placed a soft kiss on her forehead.

"I love you," she beamed with excitement.

"I love you too, baby. You and me…next month," he confirmed before walking out of her office.

The moment the closed the door, her elated smile slowly faded. She wanted to believe the man she loved, but her heart whispered otherwise. A knock sounded at her door.

"I love you, Jackson," she told herself, "but if you play me a 4th time, that's it for us." She lifted her shoulders back, stuck out her chest, held her chin high, and walked confidently over to her door to open it.

"Mr. Winston," she pleasantly extended her hand.

"Good Afternoon, Anna."

Pandora walked behind her desk and sat down. As usual, her game face was back on, "Let's get to work. What can I do for you?"

Chapter 3

Eden

"Mom, what do you think about this one?" Eden and her mother stood in the back aisle of a Babies R Us, gazing around at baby cribs.

"No," Ruby shook her head, "any color except white. Besides, it's eight hundred dollars." Lifting the price tag, Ruby double-checked the price, before flinging the tag in disgust.

"This is not the Fifties," Eden rolled her eyes. "I know back in your day cribs were only two dollars, but it's 2019 now. Eight hundred dollars is actually pretty cheap for a crib if you ask me"

"It sure is 2019, and you tacky millenials make me sick with your sense of entitlement, like the world owes you'll something," Ruby fussed. Narrowing her eyes, she shook her head at her daughter.

"And you old time hypocrites love to criticize our generation, but you forget who raised it," Eden cocked her head and shook it back at her mother.

"Eden," Ruby threatened, "please don't get choked out in this store."

"You always threaten me like I'm still a child. I'm twenty-seven-years-old. I have a degree, a car, and rights," Eden walked away from her mother to look at another crib nearby. "Besides, you wouldn't dare hit me. You're too pretty for prison," she laughed, lightening up the mood.

"I don't care if you were fifty-seven with a Ph.D and a multi-million-dollar career. You live in *my* house, don't pay *any* bills, and you're eight months pregnant with a baby that you need help raising. *My* help. Therefore, you respect me and watch your mouth, or *get out* and support yourself. And if you get smart with me one more time, you'll be picking your teeth up off the floor," Ruby declared angrily, walking over to see a cheaper crib. "*I'm too pretty for prison*," she mocked. "Ha! You want to act grown? You'll get stomped like you're grown. Leave the police out of it."

"I'm sorry, relax...*geeze*," Eden laughed. She walked over to her mother, hugging her tight. "You're gonna miss me when I'm gone. When Chris gets himself together, we're gonna get married, and when I move out with your only grandchild, you'll regret this conversation."

"You still have faith in that deadbeat?" Ruby shook her head. "Anyway, what do you think of this crib?" she changed the subject, "I like the cream color, and the shape. It's also a few hundred dollars cheaper than that other one."

"It's okay," Eden shrugged at the crib with a bitter smile, "I like the white one better. And Chris is a good man, I don't understand why you don't like him."

Ruby turned to look at her daughter. "Chris is a thirty-nine-year-old *punk,* living without a pot to piss in, or a window to throw it out of. He's messing around with girls old enough to be his daughter; *my* daughter. He's done absolutely nothing for you since you've met him other than get you pregnant. And speaking of trifling," Ruby stared down at her watch and then looked toward the front entrance, "wasn't he supposed to meet us here over an *hour* ago?"

Eden bowed her head, twiddling her fingers, "He's coming, Mom. He's just running a little late, that's all."

"Oh, for the love of-" Ruby flung her hands in the air. Though a bit fanatical, she was right. Christopher cared about noone but himself. He and Eden met while Eden was a freshman in college. Six years ago, she spotted him on campus, conversing with the dean of students as she walked with her girlfriends to the Cafeteria. She'd never had an attraction to older men, but Christopher was an exception. Her lips parted as he looked in her direction and their eyes met one another. Christopher's brown eyes had an undefinable sparkle to them. They were alluring and sensual, outlined by long, full eyelashes and a touch of mischief. They made her weak. Staring into them took her to another universe. Her girlfriends had to snap their fingers to bring her back to reality. *She had to have him.* Eden didn't care if Christopher was married, engaged, dating, or had kids, she wanted him and she told herself she wouldnt stop trying until he was hers. Luckily for her, she didn't have to try that hard. An hour later, she saw him again in the dining hall guest area. Christopher couldn't help but notice Eden's smile. She was certainly under his required age limit, but there was something about her. Traces of her innocent self lingered in her smile, and the thinness of her body. Her curves weren't fully defined yet, but she had all the trappings of womanhood. Eden's caramel skin had just the right tint of makeup, and her high heeled shoes peeked out under her frayed jeans. Her large, liquid brown eyes held such a serenity, it was almost impossible for anyone not to be mesmerized by her. As Christopher got up to leave, he walked past her table, handing her a napkin with his phone number and email address. After one phone conversation, Eden was sprung. Chris was smart, funny, and romantic, and made her feel protected, safe and cared for. Christopher also found Eden to be just as refreshing. There was a part of her that never wanted to escape her childhood. She clutched it like a purse, fearing for its safety in the adult world. Conversations with her always turned to horses, soup recipes, and music. Eden was the most childlike young adult, Chris had ever met. The world excited her. She saw opportunities ahead, a life of good fun, and good health. Chris didn't care how old Eden was, he idolized her innocence, and being with her kept him connected to his own inner boy. However, regardless of how they felt about one another, Christopher was twenty-nine, and Eden was only seventeen. They both agreed to keep their relationship to themselves. Over the entire course of her undergraduate education, Eden and Chris were head over heels in *secret love.* He'd stolen her heart, her mind, much of her time, *and* her virginity. Eden wanted so badly to share her excitement with her mother and close friends, but she knew they wouldn't accept him. As overprotective as they were, they would've had Chris arrested, and thrown *under* the jail the second they found out. Upon Graduation, Eden was offered a full scholarship to the Massachusetts Institute of Technology. When she told Christopher she'd be leaving, he was crushed.

"You're leaving me?" Chris stared down at Eden's acceptance letter, dumbfounded.

"I'll be back during breaks," she replied. "This is a once in a lifetime opportunity for me to attend MIT;

for free," she repeated herself as if he hadn't heard her the first time.

"This is also a once in a lifetime opportunity for you and me to finally make our relationship public. I had plans to propose to you and introduce you to my family."

"Chris, my mother would lose her mind if I gave up a scholarship to grad school, for some relationship. *Especially* one she knows nothing about."

"Baby, listen," Chris wrapped his arms around Eden's waist, "I want you. I want you now, and I want you forever. I've been hiding you for so long and I'm tired of it."

"I understand that," Eden replied, "I feel the same way. I've been waiting for the day to introduce you to my friends and my mother, but, what does me going to grad school have to do with it?" She asked.

"It has a lot to do with it."

"How?" Eden peered up at him, confused.

"It just does," he retorted. "Look, if grad school is important to you, then go, but I can't promise I'll be here when you get back."

Eden loved Christopher so much, that she gave up her grad school scholarship, vowing to stay behind with him. Christopher promised he'd be ready to propose to her, buy them a home, and start a family if she stayed. Two years had gone by since she finished her undergraduate studies, and none of those promises happened. The once mature, caring, respectful man that Eden had been sneaking around with, had faded into the background, as the childish, lazy, disrespectful ingrate that he really was, took form. Christopher took Eden through an array of broken promises, and continuous breakups. He changed his mind about introducing one another to their families because he felt their age difference would make him look bad. Instead of buying them a home, Chris left his rented apartment to move in with his sister. Shortly after, he was offered a job in California that would allow him to travel the world, and build a name for himself. He took the job without a second thought, broke up with Eden, and left. Eden couldn't believe his nerve. She'd sacrificed her future for him, and he played her. Eden grew depressed, her self esteem plummeted, and her positive outlook on life, love, and her education disappeared. Her mother and friends knew a boy was behind her personality change, but Eden refused to admit it. It took Ruby and Eden's friends almost a year to get Eden's priorities back in order. They begged her to go back to school, and even though Ruby was upset about a missed opportunity for a scholarship, she was still willing to pay for her daughters education out of her own pocket. Eden agreed to go. One month later she ran into Christopher, four years after he'd disappeared. He was in town for work and was so glad to see her. He took her to dinner, thoroughly apologizing over and over for his selfishness, and felt terrible for all the pain he'd caused her. After a little too much to drink, they went back to Christopher's hotel room for the ultimate apology. That one night of passion paid for a one-way ticket to motherhood, as Eden wound up pregnant.

When Eden was little, she was the apple of her father's eye and the pride and joy of her mother. Ruby owned her own hair salon, and coffee shop, which left her with a hefty income. With no other children, Ruby provided Eden with a life most young girls dreamed of. Eden on the other hand seemed to believe she was missing out on something. She loved her mother but felt like she coddled her too much. Eden had been waiting a long time to step out on her own, and be the boss of herself. The time had officially come, and it wasn't at all what she'd bargained for. *But it was too late to turn back now.*

"Listen, I know he has his flaws," Eden defended, "but I love him. You don't have to *love* him, but at least try to *like him.* He's the father of your grandchild." Ruby folded her arms. "Mom," Eden looked at her with pleading eyes.

"Yeah, at least *try* to like me, *mom.*"

Both women looked up. Christopher had walked in without either of them noticing. He winked at Eden and her mother with a playful grin.

Ruby rolled her eyes. Disgust was written all over her face. "My name is not mom, *it's Ruby.*"

"Oh, come on, I'm getting ready to give you a granddaughter, I'm a legend. It should be an honor to refer to me as your son," Chris succeeded in further annoying Ruby.

"You are no kin to me. Don't ever confuse my DNA with your own pitiful family."

Christopher stopped in his tracks and stepped back. "Ruby, you don't even know my family."

"I don't need to. I know *you.*"

"Mom," Eden gritted.

"Ever since you've come into my daughter's life, you have caused nothing but chaos," Ruby ignored her daughter, "you have ruined her education, and filled her head with a bunch of lies and promises you've never kept," her elevating voice had a few nearby shoppers looking their way. "You're sick in the head for taking advantage of a young girl."

"Mom, please...we're in *public*," Eden warned.

"Anything *else,* Miss Ruby?" Chris taunted.

Since he gave her the floor, Ruby had no problem continuing. "You're trifling, you're broke, you're immature, selfish, and not to mention *rude.*"

"Mom," Eden snapped, "I said that's enough." Eden looked around the store in embarrassment. Luckily for her, the nearby shoppers had moved onto another aisle.

"No, please, let the Jezebel continue her manipulative rant."

"Excuse me?" Ruby gawked.

Eden waddled in between them, "Guys. Come on."

"You heard me," he reiterated, "you're trying to turn Eden against me, as you've always done. You're miserable and alone, and you want her to be miserable and alone right along with you. Eden is a grown woman, and who she chooses to love is no business or decision of yours."

Eden continued to block their paths toward one another. The look of fear covered her face.

"You know what? You're right." Ruby stepped back from both of them, taking her glasses from her purse and easing them on her face. "Your love lives are none of my business. Eden, I want everything out of my house by tomorrow, or it'll be sitting on the side of the curb waiting for you...*or the garbage collector.*"

Eden snapped her head toward her mother. Her mouth dropped open.

"Why? What did *I* do?"

"This man," Ruby pointed in Christopher's direction, "this poor excuse for a man is ruining your life, one bad decision at a time. Every time he does, I'm here to pick up your broken pieces. Now, its time for you to deal with your decisions on your own. Hopefully, the lessons you learn in this will serve as a permanent reminder not to get yourself involved with any more junk like this."

"Kiss my ass, lady," Christopher fussed back, offended.

"Chris, stop it," Eden shouted.

"My sentiments exactly," Ruby shook her head before storming out of the store.

"Mom, wait," Eden yelled, "oh my gosh, Chris, why do you always have to go back and forth with her?"

"Whatever. She's just upset, she's not gonna put you out," he spoke confidently.

"And if she does? Where am I gonna go? Is there room at your sister's house for me *and* a baby?"

"No, but we can put you in a hotel until we figure it out."

"A hotel?" Eden turned her face up, "why can't we just get our own place?"

"Eden, you know I can't afford that right now, don't start with this today…We'll figure something out. Your baby shower is this Saturday anyway. Isn't she planning it?"

"*My* baby shower? You mean *our* baby shower."

"No, I meant *yours*. I don't have to be there, do I?" He said, slightly agitated.

"What do you mean? *Yes,* you have to be there!"

Chris sighed loudly. "This is too much. I don't want to go to some ridiculous event full of women, and girly games."

"You can't be serious right now," Eden couldn't believe it. "This is an event to welcome our child into the world. How can you be so selfish?"

"There you go, sounding like your mother," he huffed.

Eden turned on her heels to walk out. She wasn't going to let him add to the bad day she was already having. "I'll talk to you later," she began waddling out of the store.

"Where are you going? You had me rush all the way here to pick out furniture."

"Well, you pissed off my mother and burned that bridge, so I don't have any money for baby furniture. And your attitude towards our baby shower isn't assuring at all. I have a dinner date with my friends, I'll talk to you later tonight."

"Fine by me. Call me when you get over yourself," Chris turned away without hesitation, and walked out."

Eden was left standing in the middle of the aisle. Reaching into her purse, she grabbed her phone to call an Uber. She was expecting her first child, and this was supposed to be a happy time for her. *Sadly, things were far from it.*

Chapter 4

Quinn, Eden, and Pandora sat in a crowded Olive Garden restaurant, nibbling on breadsticks. It'd been a month since they'd seen each other, and for a close-knit friendship like the one they had, that was a *long* time. Pandora and Quinn had been friends since elementary school. They became enemies for a season after Pandora's brother, Joseph, was pounded by Andre for trying to kiss Quinn behind the bleachers during gym in middle school. Their friendship rekindled 3 months later after Quinn shared her last piece of bubble gum with Pandora during third period science.

When Pandora and Quinn were fourteen, they went with their mothers to Ms. Ruby's coffee shop for breakfast. While there, they met Ruby's daughter; nine-year-old Eden. Eden was in such awe of Pandora and Quinn at first glance. Quinn had the kindest pair of stormy gray eyes, trimmed by long, gorgeous lashes. She had florid cheeks and flawlessly sculpted lips. Pandora had a borne arrogance and the sassiest attitude, but she was so warm toward Eden, Eden wanted to be her friend anyway. Quinn and Pandora found Eden's youthful shyness, and bright eyes, absolutely adorable. Her cheeks were flushed and her curls did such a lively dance when she talked. From the moment they met Eden, they loved her. The three of them turned out to be the best of friends.

Growing up, they shared the happiest moments of their lives together. There was laughter; *what a shrill chorus they made*. When they weren't together, they texted and talked on the phone daily. Their teenage years were filled with shopping, endless sleepovers, boyfriend meltdowns, learning to drive a car, and hanging out at the mall. The three of them grew up so beautifully, remaining inseparable until after undergrad when Quinn attended grad school in New York, Pandora went to Law school in Philadelphia, and Eden stayed behind in Virginia. As the years passed, how *different* the three of them became, as all the softness of childhood was replaced by sharp edges and chiseled lines. Quinn and Pandora were now thirty-three years old, at the top of their professional careers, while Eden was twenty-seven, anxiously awaiting motherhood. It never mattered how hard life got, with one another, they were the softest version of themselves, *free to just be*. They held pieces of each other's hearts everywhere they went, protecting it with their lives.

"What a shame for us to come here for years, solely for the breadsticks," Pandora chuckled.

"What an even bigger shame that no one's caught on to us after 5 years," Eden stuffed her mouth full of buttery bread. Quinn nibbled at the bread like she thought it was poisoned.

"I'm trying to shed a few pounds for the summer, and you guys bring me here of all places."

"Shed a few pounds where?" Pandora looked at Quinn like she had three heads.

"Between her ears, I suppose," Eden teased.

"Please, with the constant traveling and eating out Andre and I have been doing for the last two months, I've put on about ten pounds."

"And you're still drop-dead gorgeous," Pandora jealously shook her head.

"Yup. To this day, men still trip over their own two feet at the sight of you just like they did when we were younger," Eden chuckled.

"I don't know, I think Anna's got me beat," Quinn laughed, "remember that guy in Spain that eye stalked her for three hours at the airport?"

"Oh my goodness," Pandora shuddered," I still get nightmares every time I think about his creepy stare."

"Well, we know Quinn is easy to like, but I don't know why men like *you* so much," Eden looked at Pandora, amused.

"What can I say? I've been blessed with beauty," Pandora replied.

"Correction. We*'ve* been blessed with beauty," Eden pointed to herself and Quinn, "you've been *cursed* with it. Your strut, your smile, those dimples-you use it all as weapons in the courtroom to manipulate the prosecutor and distract the jury to win your cases…" Eden shook her head, "and they fall for it everytime. If they only knew how callous you really were."

"Callous?" Pandora mocked, playfully.

"I disagree. I don't think your looks would alter whether you won or lost a case" Quinn defended, "you'll *always* be the queen of the courtroom."

"Touche," Eden affirmed, "still, every night I pray for boils or an accident, maybe that way you'll rejoin humanity someday."

"You're *so* lucky your pregnant," Pandora replied. The three of them burst into laughter.

"I cannot wait to rid myself of this luck," Eden rubbed her belly, "I feel like I've been pregnant forever."

"Really? You seemed to be enjoying the process," Pandora replied.

"I was- but a few days ago that *feeling* arrived."

"What feeling?" Quinn looked confused.

"The feeling all mothers in their last trimester feel; that they're gonna be pregnant forever. And it's really bizarre because I'm an intelligent woman, and know for a fact I can't be pregnant forever," she laughed at herself, "but that's how over this trimester I am."

"You wear it so well, though," Pandora replied,

"your skin is radiant, your hair grew, your nails look healthier, isn't she stunning, Quinn?"

As Pandora spoke, Quinn just looked at her as if she were a radio, instead of a person to be interacted with. Quinn swallowed hard, her mind temporarily paralyzed. Seeing her best friend pregnant was a bittersweet feeling. After all, *she* was the one everyone looked up too. Everyone created their fairytale through watching Quinn and Andre over the years. It was because of their love that people still believed in its magic. *And magical it was.* First came love, then came marriage, but year after year there was no baby carriage. Quinn could distinctly remember the first few years her and Andre tried to get pregnant. She was so excited to start a new chapter in their lives. She didn't really have any worries about it working, it was just a matter of when. Maybe not the first try, but within a few months she was sure she would get pregnant. Her and Andre were in their 20's, and in great health, so she didn't think they'd run into a problem. One year and thirty-three negative pregnancy tests later, *Quinn knew there was a problem.* She thought *having* the baby was the hard part, not *conceiving* it. Over the years, everyone around her seemed to get pregnant naturally. There was always someone posting a pregnancy announcement, or a photo of a baby being born on Facebook. Quinn was happy for them, but it was a constant reminder of her own situation. When Eden conceived, it hurt to hear Eden tell her and Pandora it was accidental and unplanned. Quinn watched Eden force herself to come to terms with having a baby on the way, and there she was, waiting patiently for it to happen to her, knowing she'd be so thankful when it did. *It never did.*

"Quinn, are you alright?" Quinn snapped out of her thoughts to see Eden and Pandora staring at her, concerned.

"I'm sorry, my mind went back to my office," she lied, "Eden, you look absolutely stunning. It'll all be over soon, keep hanging in there."

"I'm trying," Eden assured. "Anyhow, what's going on with you two?"

"Nothing too exciting," Quinn lied a second time. *There was no need for her friends to know her marriage was hanging on by a thread these days.* "Anna, how's your fiancé?"

"It's not her fiancé anymore, it's her boyfriend," Eden blurted.

"I'm sure they're engaged again," Quinn laughed. Eden joined in.

"He is my fiancé again, *thank you*," Pandora rolled her eyes before she took another bite of her bread.

"Sure. For how long *this* time?" Eden asked.

"Next month, actually," Pandora stated, matter-of-factly, "we're getting married on the beach in Puerto Rico."

Eden and Quinn paused like a game of freeze. They looked at one another and then back at Pandora.

"You're joking, right?" Eden furrowed. The air in the room grew so thick, you could cut it with a knife. Pandora knew her friends didn't approve of Jackson. They had yet to meet him, and quite frankly they weren't interested in doing so. Jackson barely had time for her, so being social like normal people was definitely reaching.

"No, I'm not joking, and for his sake he'd better not be either," Pandora let her guard down and lowered her head. "You don't have to say it, it's silly to keep getting on and off his merry go round, I know."

"So why do you keep getting *on and off?*" Quinn asked softly, "why do you continue to be in a relationship that makes a mockery of your pride, values, and self-esteem?"

"Love...that's why. I mean, I don't know," Pandora responded like a senior in high school.

"That's not a good enough answer," Quinn responded sternly. "The last time I checked, you were the third best defense attorney in the country. You don't even take lip from the judge."

"The courtroom and the bedroom are two different places," Pandora mumbled.

"Ah...So good sex is the stone that brings down Goliath?" Quinn raised an eyebrow. "Anna, at some point, you're gonna have to accept the reality you already know and move forward."

"I know," Pandora sighed, "I can't really pinpoint why I keep folding for his antics, but it's getting old.

If he doesn't keep his promise next month, I'm done. For good this time," she assured.

"Well, you're not the only fool in love. I'm going through the same thing with Chris," Eden chimed in.

"He's still acting up?" Pandora asked.

"Is he? He got into it with my mother earlier in Babies R Us. She was so pissed, she kicked *me* out of her house for it." Pandora gasped. Quinn buried her face in her hands.

"There has got to be a spell or something we can place on these men to get them to behave," Eden said, just as the waitress approached the table.

"Is there anything else I can get for you ladies today?" she asked politely.

"No, we're fine, just the check. Thank you," Pandora replied.

"Not a problem," the waitress smiled and walked off.

"I think the real question to be asked is, why do you'll allow these broken men into your lives?" Quinn intervened. "I mean, sure, nobody's perfect, but my *goodness*, the disrespect on their part is crushing. And both of you have collectively invented every excuse for staying."

"Not to mention, I think we've gotten pretty creative about it over the years," Pandora shook her head and laughed at herself.

"They keep giving you every reason to leave, and you keep ignoring them. I don't understand, and I'm the psychologist," Quinn motioned.

"Think about you and Andre for a second," Pandora looked at Quinn, "you guys are like friendship set on fire," Pandora smiled just thinking about it. "Your love is one for the ages. To be in your husbands arms must feel like safety, freedom, and passion. We've seen Andre bring you back to life, revive what you lost, and restore what was shattered. You two were *born* to love. Now, imagine if he betrayed your affections and left your heart in a shattered disarray of pieces. What if he stole so many pieces of you, it became almost impossible to put yourself back together? Would you leave him?" A tear flooded Pandora's eyes before she quickly wiped it away. "Leaving would be the right thing to do, right? Or would you stick around in hopes that he would return what he stole so all can be well again?" Quinn bit down on her lower lip as her eyes turned glossy with tears. Pandora had taken a page straight out of her reality. She didn't need to take an educated guess as to how she would feel, she was a living witness. Immediately, Quinn tried to blink her emotions away, but a tear slipped through anyhow. She managed to fake a grin that buried her pain deep in her heart. Her friends saw something flash beneath the surface of her smile. They both hurried to investigate her sudden shift, but Quinn was quick. Before either of them could gather their thoughts, Quinn's emotions disappeared before they could identify it. *The beauty of a psychologist.*

Eden's ringing cellphone interrupted their moment. She glanced at it and saw it was her mother. Rolling her eyes, she ignored the call.

"My mom really needs to make up her mind about the choices she makes."

"Was that her you just ignored?" Pandora asked, amused.

"It sure was. She just threw me out of the house less than an hour ago, and then she texted me to inquire if I was alright about it," Pandora and Quinn burst into laughter. "I'm serious. Of course, I ignored her text message so now she's calling me."

"Miss Ruby loves you, I highly doubt she'd put you out for real, she's just trying to teach you a lesson," Pandora implied.

"Who knows, but I know for *certain* she's not hosting my baby shower this Saturday. I doubt if she even comes, knowing Chris will be there."

Quinn's face fell faster than a corpse in cement boots.

"It's *this* Saturday?"

"Yes, the twenty-fifth. Please don't tell me you're not coming," Eden looked worried.

"Oh no, I have it in my calendar as the following Saturday. I have to do a woman's conference this weekend. I'm *so* sorry," Quinn's eyes lowered, and her shoulders slumped. She felt terrible.

"You guys, this is *really* important to me. You two are my closest friends," Eden looked disappointed. She could've cared less if no one else came to her baby shower, but the thought of her best friend missing her special day left a huge lump in her throat. She was dying for them to meet Christopher, and with their busy schedules and hardened hearts toward him, there was never a right time. Her baby shower was the perfect place.

"I'll make it up for the both of us," Pandora's face lit up. "What if I hosted the shower in place of Miss. Ruby?"

"You'd do that for me?" Eden's eyes lit up. Quinn thought to herself briefly.

"The women's retreat is from Friday night, to Saturday evening, but if I can sneak off during the day,

I will. And, whatever you don't get from your guests, I'll see to it that you get it," she promised.

"Wow, thank you guys so much," Eden smiled.

"No thanks, needed. I'm excited to meet Mr. *Douchebag* anyway," Pandora squinted, mischievously.

"*Anna*", Quinn warned, "please don't go in there and embarrass that man in front of the world," Quinn warned.

"I know, I know, don't worry," Pandora laughed. Quinn looked at her cell phone and quickly grabbed her purse.

"I'm gonna get going, I'm late for a meeting with a client." Taking out a 20 dollar bill, she placed it on the table.

"No problem, we're gonna head out in a little bit too," Pandora replied, as Quinn reached down and kissed their foreheads."See you soon."

Chapter 5

Andre stood in the pulpit of his Mega church, gazing out at the seventy-five women on the women's ministry that he'd called to a meeting. Tabernacle was a beautiful church, old stoned and stained glass, but to Andre, it was just a cage for religion that was passed down to him from his parents. God couldn't be contained by walls, but he had a legacy to fulfill, so he opted to leave a good imprint. Andre often wondered how his parents made things look so easy. There were finances to be handled, ministries to oversee, and the women. *There were so many women.* While many of them kept their secret fantasies to themselves, there were some bold ones who made their hidden agendas public. From the love notes on Andre's car, attached to his windshield, to the threats to beat down Quinn and nail her to the oversized wooden cross above the large pulpit window, Pastor Bentley had his work cut out for him. Although some of the women were beautiful, he knew who he was married to, and he respected his union and honored his vows. Lately, however, with things not quite right at home, Andre's focus began to shift, and his eyes started to wander.

"Thank you all for showing up tonight," he spoke, "I apologize for our building expansion project limiting the church's use for rehearsals and events this weekend, but we'll have everything up and running soon. Does anyone have any questions or concerns for me before we dismiss?"

"I do," Diamond, a stripper, turned born again believer sat in the front row with a white, form-fitting dress that exposed her sun-kissed, triple D cleavage, stood to her feet. "If all of our weekend activities are canceled, what about the women's conference?"

"I believe that's still going on," he replied, "First Lady booked another venue. I'm sure she'll reach out to the committee as soon as things are finalized."

"Is she here at all?" Diamond asked with a mischievous grin, fluttering her eyes in a way that only Andre could notice. Diamond studied him. She'd been doing so very blatantly these days, and realized she was beginning to become a distraction for him. As she flirted from her seat, Andre couldn't help but glance at her beautifully toned legs. She relaxed her body back into the wooden pew, her eyes locked on him as she crossed her legs to give him a better view.

"She had a previous engagement this afternoon," Andre cleared his throat. He hadn't spoken to Quinn all day, and he knew after the way they left one another this morning, there was no way Quinn would step foot in his presence.

"Well...Since the First Lady isn't here, I—"

"First Lady is right here," everyone in the room focused on the side stage door where Quinn had just entered. She walked in gracefully, yet confident. Her heels clicked on the hardwood floor as she walked to her seat on the pulpit.

Andre turned to her. He was shocked that she actually made it out. "Hi, Baby, you made it. We were just asking for you."

"Were you?" Quinn asked.

"Sister Diamond had questions about the women's conference this weekend, and wanted to know if it was still going on," he passed Quinn the microphone.

"Yes, the conference is still on, ladies," she smiled. "Since we can't use the church anymore, I was able to secure us a space at the Radisson Hotel, in Richmond. If anyone needs a ride, there will be a bus leaving from the Church at 3pm sharp on Friday," she glared at Diamond. "Does that answer your question, *Sister Diamond?*"

Quinn was far from oblivious of Diamond's hidden intentions. The poisonous stare she gave her let Diamond know she knew it.

"Yes…" Diamond replied dryly, "Thank you."

Snickers from a few of the woman could be heard throughout the room.

"Well then," Andre cut through the awkward silence, "I guess we'll see everyone here on Sunday. You're dismissed."

The women got up from their seats and walked through different exits. Andre glanced to his left to see Diamond exiting the building. Her round buttocks stuck out like two volleyballs, as she strutted to the door. Instantly, he was aroused.

"Pastor," one of the deacons called, breaking Andre's stare, "we're gonna lock up downstairs. We'll be by the back door waiting for you, and First Lady to exit your office."

"Right," he cleared his thoughts, "okay. No problem." He walked over to Quinn, who was headed out of the pulpit door. Adjusting his posture, he wiped the lude thoughts of Diamond from his memory.

"This was a surprise," he grinned.

Quinn turned to him. "My six o'clock appointment canceled at the last minute. I had some free time, so I decided to stop by," she clutched her purse and looked around the sanctuary, refusing to look directly at her husband.

"Well, I'm glad you did," he moved in closer to her.

Quinn moved backward.

"No problem...I'll see you at home, then," her cold, bitter tone sent shivers through his body. Andre could feel the venom pouring off of her as she turned to leave.

"Baby, wait," he pleaded.

Quinn didn't budge. She exited out of the pulpit and into her husband's office. Andre followed closely behind her, closing his office door once they were in. Leaning against the door, he used both of his hands to pull Quinn into him, her back still in view.

Quinn stood there, emotionless.

"I'm sorry about earlier," he wrapped his arms around his wife. The guilt he felt was like gasoline in his guts. The things he'd said to her couldn't be undone. It squeezed at his brain, obliterating his ego. The scene from their bedroom replayed in Quinn's mind as well, as she wiped away her onset of tears.

"I didn't mean to-"

"It's fine," she stared at the wall across the office.

"It's *not* fine. Look at me," Andre spun Quinn in his direction. Gazing at her angelic face, he instantly grew disgusted at himself. Quinn was the queen of façades, but Andre could see right through it. Her pain was evident in the crease of her brow, and the down curve of her lips. And her eyes, they showed her soul. They were a deep pool of restless gray, an ocean of hopeless grief. Her eyes shifted, becoming glazed with a glassy layer of tears. As Quinn blinked, they slid from her eyelids and dripped down her cheeks. Biting her lip, she attempted to hide any sound that wanted out of her mouth. *Andre's heart sank.*

"I'm sorry I hurt you- hurt us," he corrected himself, "it's not you, alright? It's me. I've been going through a lot over the last six months. We should've talked a long time ago, but I got caught up in my ego and lost in the glorification of being busy. This isn't fair to you."

"I don't understand, "Quinn replied softly, as Andre used his finger to wipe her tears, "what could possibly be wrong, that you're afraid to talk to me about? We've always tackled our personal problems together."

"I know. I guess I just wanted to try and tackle this one on my own. But I failed. Listen, after the Women's retreat this weekend, can you schedule the week off?" he touched her hands, "I'll put the assistant Pastor in charge. Let's go away somewhere, just us so we can talk, and pick our marriage back up. Does that sound promising?"

"It does," she nodded. Quinn and Andre seemed to have a silent conversation as they stared into each other's eyes. Beneath their talk was the love, the gentle gaze of their eyes, and the relaxed nature of their faces. It spoke of a love that lay between them, ancient and timeless. Andre leaned in, kissing Quinn softly, with a kiss that felt just right. *Once. Twice. Three times.* Quinn smiled and kissed him back. Without warning, Andre clutched Quinn into his arms, pulling her into a fiery, passionate kiss, and who was she to stop him? He was her drug of choice. She was addicted to him. He'd betrayed her affections, and left her heart in disarray, yet she was still in love with him and ready to forgive him at the drop of a dime. As he ran his hands up her arms, electricity shot through her heart. Quinn and Andre were born to love one another. Her hands worked their way around his body, feeling along his perfect physique over his suit. With the office door closed, every pretense fell. The facade they showed the world in the form of Pastor, and First Lady melted away. They kissed each other with a raw intensity- breathing fast, hearts beating faster. Before Quinn knew it, she was slammed against the office door, half naked, as their skin moved softly together. *At least it started off soft.* Somewhere along the way, lines were crossed, and the rhythm of love shifted into lust as Diamond took over the forefront of Andre's mind. Over the last two months, Diamond wouldn't leave him alone. She popped up at the most vulnerable moments, wore the tightest clothes, and gave him the most lustful gazes. Quinn opened her eyes. With each dirty thought of pleasing another woman, Andre got rougher and rougher. His grip on her waist made Quinn squeal in pain. Through narrowed eyes, she stared at him and frowned, searching her husband's face for passion and meaning, but all she saw was a perverted lust. Andre used every inch of flesh God gave him to dig into Quinn's womanhood.

Baby, let's stop, you're hurting me," she begged, trying to twist her body off of him.

Andre refused. He held her tighter and kissed her rougher.

"Andre," she repeated. Still, no response. He was stuck in some kind of lustful trance that was pleasing to him, but excruciating to her.

"Stop!" She wailed, as a surge of pain shot through her insides. Quinn used her leg to knee him in the side. The pain caused his legs to buckle. Losing his balance, he tumbled to the floor with Quinn on top of him. She quickly threw herself off of him and crawled away.

"What is *wrong* with you?" She looked terrified. A hard knock sounded at his door.

"Pastor, everything alright in there?" A Deacon's voice sounded, "we're waiting to lock up."

Andre snapped out of his fantasy. His eyes grew wider when he looked at his wife a few feet away.

"Baby…" he scrambled to his feet, fixing his pants before hurrying over to help her up.

"Don't touch me," Quinn got up from the floor and backed away from him.

"Quinn," he hissed.

Pastor?" The Deacon called.

Andre walked over to the door to crack it open. "Everything is *fine,* Deacon, we'll be right out."

"My apologies, I didn't hear you. Just making sure everyone is safe,"

"Just give us a couple more minutes," Andre nodded his head and closed the door quickly. He turned back to his wife. "Quinn. I'm sor—"

Quinn was gone. He glanced at the back door just in time to see it close.

Chapter 6

"I can't believe I volunteered myself for this," Pandora teetered on a chair in the clubhouse of Ruby's condominium development, as she hung a pink banner on the wall. The day of Eden's baby shower had finally come, but Pandora wasn't prepared at all. Her feeling sorry for Eden over dinner caused her to open her big mouth and commit to hosting an event she knew nothing about. A cease and desist order, she could do. Interior decorating? Not so much. Over the next hour and a half, she struggled through hanging banners, streamers, and setting the tables. When the last streamer was placed, she got down and surveyed the room. Just as she walked over to the nearest table and grabbed the handmade centerpieces, Ruby emerged in the doorway, carrying a big plastic bag full of her own decorations. She stopped at the entrance when she noticed an unfamiliar figure.

"And you are?" Ruby lowered her chin to her chest.

Pandora placed the centerpiece on the table and smiled to herself, before spinning around to face Ruby with one hand on her hip...

"Hi, Miss Ruby. I see you haven't changed," she laughed, displaying a wide grin.

Ruby's mouth fell open. She flung her arms in the air and slapped her hands against her cheeks, letting the bag she held fall to the floor in front of her.

"Oh my goodness, *Pandora!*" She shouted cheerfully, rushing to embrace Pandora with a firm hug and kiss.

"How are you, baby? It's been years since I've seen you."

"I'm wonderful, just like you I see," Pandora chuckled.

"You look amazing," Ruby's eyes traveled up and down Pandora's figure. "I see you on the news all the time dealing with the press and pulling cold-blooded criminals out of the fire."

"Yes, Ma'am…that's me," she replied,

Ruby walked back to the doorway to retrieve her bags, "Eden must've told you about our little argument this week. I'm assuming that's why she has you here setting up, because she figured I wouldn't be here."

"She did," Pandora confirmed, "but now that you *are* here, feel free to take over." Grabbing the scotch tape from a nearby table, Pandora walked over and handed it to Ruby. "I don't mind hosting, but this decorating stuff is not my thing."

"Of course I'll take over," Ruby laughed, taking the tape. "I'm not *that* bad of a mother to cancel on a welcome party for my first grandchild. *Even if I don't like her poor excuse for a father"*

Pandora turned, trying to conceal her laugh. She headed up to the stage to set up the microphones.

"I'm serious," Ruby continued, "he makes me sick to my stomach. Have you ever met him? Am I the only one that can't stand him?"

"I've never met him," Pandora admitted, "I honestly don't care to, after some of the things I've heard. *But,* if he's going to be here for a while, I guess there's no time like the present. Still, it doesn't matter what my feelings are toward him, Eden is crazy in love with him, and I have to respect it."

"I guess that's the mature route to take," Ruby moved to another table to set her party favors on it. "It just disappoints me as a mother. I didn't raise her to be so naïve, and careless with her heart."

"Don't look at it like that. You're a *great* mother. Don't beat yourself up about something you can't control. Eden is grown and will love who she wants. As her friends, Quinn and I are just here to catch her when she falls. I think you should join us. Some people only learn through experience," Pandora winked.

"Quinn..." Ruby looked up from the table and smiled. "How is she? I havent seen her in almost a year. She's always on that Gospel network, sitting alongside that fine husband of hers."

"She's great," Pandora stepped off the stage, "Still flawless. Still saving the world. Still...Quinn."

"That's my girl. I always knew she'd do big things, someday. What about you? Are you still crazy?" Ruby asked with a side eye.

"When I need to be," Pandora smirked, "for the most part, I'm just enjoying my career. But...I'm engaged." She dangled her three-carat, princess cut diamond in Ruby's direction.

Ruby gasped. "That's beautiful," she adjusted her glasses to get a better view. "When is the wedding, and when do I get to meet this lucky fellow? What's his name? What's he like?"

Pandora tilted her head back and laughed, "His name is Jackson. We've been engaged off and on, for a while now. He's an accountant, so he travels a lot; at least 4 times per month. Our relationship has been *so* unstable over the last few years, but I feel like we're finally getting some consistency. See, Eden's not the only one with man problems," Pandora giggled. "Anyhow, after a long talk about love and commitment, we've decided to get married next month in Puerto Rico."

Ruby was ecstatic. She covered her opened mouth with both hands, muffling her squeals. "Wonderful, just wonderful. God is so good. I remember when all three of you snot-nosed little girls used to sit on my front porch and giggle about love, and boys. Look at you all now," Ruby smiled.

"Those were the good ole' days," Pandora said. "Before love, menstrual cycles, and responsibility came along."

When the first few arrivals came strolling in, Pandora glanced at her watch. "Oh, it's 3 o'clock already. I should start greeting folks. Do you need any more help?"

"No, no. I'm fine, this is my last table. You go ahead."

Just as Pandora stepped back up on the stage, her phone began to vibrate. Pulling it from her pocket, she glanced at the screen.

"Hello, all," she smiled at the incoming party guests, "you can put your gifts on the gift table, to the left by the cake. Sit anywhere you'd like," she announced, tapping the green accept button on her iPhone.

"Hello?"

"Anna, where are you? I've been calling you all afternoon," Jackson blurted, without even a hello.

"Jackson, please, you called me *one* time, and I was busy. I tried calling you back, and you didn't answer…just like you didn't answer me all day yesterday, and the day before that."

"I called you four times, Pandora. "Your phone kept sending me to voicemail," he fussed.

Pandora rolled her eyes and looked at her watch again. "What do you want, Jackson? I'm busy."

"I just wanted to hear your voice and tell you I love you. I'll be in town in a few days. I plan on spending them with you, instead of a hotel."

"Hmmm. We'll see."

"Why do you have to be so negative all the time?" He sounded frustrated. "I haven't spoken to you in *two* days."

"That's the point. We're getting ready to be married in less than thirty days, and these disappearing acts you promised would stop, *haven't* changed yet."

Ruby walked over to Pandora and tapped her on her shoulder, "We're ready to start," she motioned with her lips, giving Pandora a smile and a thumbs up. Pandora nodded.

"I told you last week I was going to Dallas," Jackson stated, "the towers here are crap, so I haven't been able to talk much, and the internet—"

"Jackson," she cut him off, "I have to go. We'll talk later."

"Wow…just like that?"

"Goodbye," she shook her head, ending the call. She slipped her phone into her back pocket and looked up to see Eden standing behind the doorway, waving at her. Her dark brown, Brazilian weave was now highlighted in different shades of brown, and her long, white, backless maxi dress hugged her tiny body, and big belly. *She looked gorgeous.* Pandora's eyes lit up, hurrying to the back doorway to greet her friend.

"Eden!"

"Everything looks so beautiful," Eden squealed, peaking into the room.

Pandora grabbed the door, pulling it shut. "No peeking until it's time to walk in." Pandora looked over Eden, glancing around the hallway. "Where's douchebag?" She laughed.

"*Christopher* is parking the car and is on his way up now. Please be nice," Eden begged.

"I was only kidding," Pandora smiled, "*I'll* be nice. Your mother? Not so much."

"My *mom* is here?" Eden gasped in fright.

"She is…but, we talked…hopefully it helped. We should get started. I'm gonna go start everything, and announce you guys so you can walk in together."

Pandora blew her a kiss and walked into the room, shutting the double doors behind her. She took her time walking to the stage as she waved and smiled at the dozens of guests who filled the room. Stepping on to the platform, she picked up a microphone.

"Thank you everyone, for coming this afternoon," she began, "I'm—"

"Joanna Wilson. That defense attorney from the Pickett case," a guest hollered in excitement.

"That's right," Pandora winked.

"How in the world did you pull that off, and still be able at sleep at night?" Another guest shook her head, disgusted.

"Guys, come on," Ruby furrowed, "We're here for a baby shower, not a press conference."

"Thank you, Miss Ruby," Pandora smiled, before continuing. "In addition to my love for criminal law, I also have a love for Eden. She's been my best friend for a long time now. When we were younger, we always joked about who would be the first to have children. She swore she'd beat us to the punch, and she certainly did," Pandora giggled. "I'm a little older than she is, so I've had the opportunity to watch her grow through every milestone of her life. I was there for grade school graduations and all of her proms. My busy schedule forced me to miss her college graduation, but Miss Ruby had me on Skype the entire time. Now, she's getting ready to bring her first *baby* into the world, and I get to be here for it."

Ruby watched from afar with a big smile painted on her face. Pandora swiped at her watery eyes.

"I'm so proud of the woman she's become. Can we all just stand in celebrating this beautiful, mother to be, and the man she loves?" The audience stood to their feet, cheering with glee. Ruby threw her hands into the air, waving them wildly with a smile so big, all thirty-two of her teeth showed. As Eden and Christopher entered into the clubhouse, the entire room exploded with joy.

The crowd was full of close family members, and childhood friends, overtaken with joy to be present for the transformation of a woman into a mother. Everyone loved Eden, and it did them proud to see her doing well. Pandora smiled and grinned, using every ounce of power in her lungs to let Eden know how appreciative she was, and would always be. Eden had a slew of support behind her. *Surely, she would be just fine.*

Suddenly, Pandora's clapping began to fade, and her smile froze in place. Her screams of excitement got lost in the back of her throat, as did her breathing. Her eyes locked on a target, yet, what she saw, no-one else could see. Her brain started to shut down, and her hands trembled so much, the microphone she held, fell to the floor. She stood there completely dumbfounded for what felt like an eternity, trapped in her own psychosis, *a living nightmare for one*. She stared at Christopher as if he were a ghost. Finally, she managed to scream,

"JACKSON!?"

Chapter 7

The deafening shrill of Pandora's scream stopped Jackson in his tracks. When he looked up and saw Pandora, his face became just as immobile as the rest of his body. Eden held his hand, continuing her walk toward the stage until her body jolted to a halt, due to Jackson's inability to move.

"Anna?" Jackson muttered. Eden noticed Pandora's face and turned to see Christopher with the same expression.

"What's wrong?" She asked, her head rotating between the two. Jackson couldn't respond, or even acknowledge Eden if he wanted to, as Pandora's eyes held him prisoner right where he stood. Her chilling grimace was enough to send demons running for cover. The crowd's applause began mellowing out, as people began to wonder what the problem was. Pandora paid them no mind. The entire room had now become a meaningless backdrop, *a mere stage for the drama to come.*

"I didn't know you knew my fiancé, Eden. What a surprise…" Pandora folded her arms.

"Fiancé? Who?" Eden looked startled.

Ruby watched from afar, putting the pieces of the puzzle together. The air seemed to get thinner by the second as Jackson stood there, experiencing his worst nightmare coming to life.

"Baby…" He finally swallowed the knot in his throat, "let me explain."

"*Baby*?" Eden snapped her head at Christopher, "*what* is going on? Anna, this is *Christopher*, my boyfriend since college."

"No...His name is Jackson Ford, and he's been my fiancé for the last nine months," Pandora bared her teeth at him.

The crowd gasped. Whispers began filling the room.

"What!?" Eden hollered with a pinched expression.

Jackson's palms started to sweat. If it was possible for him to just drop dead at will, he would have, in that moment.

"Eden...I..." he stumbled over his words in search of something to say. "Can we...let's go outside and talk."

Some say you find love's purpose in the simplicity of your heartbeat. Pandora placed her hand on her chest. She knew she had a one, but she couldn't feel it beating anymore. She looked away and then looked back to see if her reality was still there. *It was.*

"No-no, how about we talk right here," Pandora roared. Picking up the black microphone, she threw it at Jackson's face in a fit of rage. Her arm was on point. The microphone hit him between his eyes. Jackson leaned back, grabbing his face in pain.

"*Uh oh*," an elderly woman sitting close by, gasped. Everyone in the room watched the scene as if they were in a theater.

"I thought you were in *Texas* with a *client*, you lying, son of a-"

"Anna, I need you to—"

Before Jackson could finish, Pandora threw the microphone stand in his direction, followed by a wooden stool from a grand piano on the stage. Jackson made every attempt to dodge it, but he wasn't fast enough. The stool crashed into his face like a car wreck, causing him to buckle over in pain.

"Pandora, *stop*," Eden screamed.

Pandora's face had *pissed* written all over it. There was no stopping her. *Not now.* She lunged at Jackson with her fists, trying to beat him down like he stole something. The only thing Jackson could do was block her hits with one hand, and cover his bleeding nose with the other.

"*Jesus*," Ruby hissed. She, along with several others rushed over to help.

"I played your stupid game, and believed all of your ridiculous lies!" Pandora roared, "I had a feeling something wasn't right, but I had no idea it had amounted to something like this." Ruby came from behind and gripped Pandora by her waist, pulling her off of Jackson.

"Anna, I guarantee you *somebody* in here is recording on their cell phone. If you're not going to consider his life, at *least* consider your career," Ruby threatened.

"This is *not* happening to me," Eden repeated to herself, hyperventilating.

"How does this happen?" Pandora screamed, before turning to face Eden. "This...*That's* the Christopher you've been dating since college? The one who supposedly lives with his sister? The one you said couldn't support you, because he can't support himself?"

"That's him," Ruby confirmed,

"This is absurd. This man owns a multimillion-dollar business, as an accountant. *My* accountant handles all of his books, so he's not lying about his income."

The crowd went into a frenzy. Everyone looked at Jackson, awaiting a response.

Eden quickly stormed out of the hall and began to cry. Her cousin got up and ran behind her. Jackson looked back at Pandora like a deer in headlights. Pandora was so disgusted, she wanted to spit in his face, and slap her own self. She's *lawyer* for crying out loud. *A good one.* She could spot a liar from a mile away, and had an IQ to the stratosphere. How could something like this go unnoticed, right under her nose for so long? *A stupid genius.* Breaking free from Ruby's grasp, Pandora rushed to her purse and snatched out her .32 caliber, semi-automatic pistol. *Somebody was going to pay for her humiliated, broken heart.*

"Anna, put that away," Ruby yelled. The rest of the crowd panicked. Jackson stared at Pandora, and then down at her gun. His eyes were so big, they nearly bulged out of their sockets. If anyone was bold enough to send a bullet straight through his head in broad daylight, amongst a crowd full of people at a baby shower and not even blink twice about it, *it was Pandora.*

"Anna, calm down, this isn't what it looks like- I," the sound of her gun cocking, cut him off. This was not a game, and this was a not a false alarm. *She was going to shoot him. Without hesitation.* The entire room screamed, scattering like roaches as Jackson raced for the emergency exits with the rest of the guests. Just as Pandora put her finger on the trigger, Eden's aunt rushed over from behind and pushed her as hard as she could. Losing her balance, Pandora stumbled to the ground, as her gun hit the floor. Eden stood at bay, her lips curled in disbelief. The scene was quite unbelievable, shocking really. Her mind reeled, unable to comprehend or process the images it was being sent by her eyes. Rushing back into the clubhouse to ensure her mother was okay, she tripped over a centerpiece that had fallen on the floor. Losing her balance, Eden went soaring into the carpet.

Ruby rushed to her rescue before she hit the floor, belly first.

"Eden, be careful," Ruby scrambled in a panic. She grabbed Eden's arm and helped her to her feet.

"Pandora, what is *wrong* with you?" Eden shouted.

"She's losing her mind," Ruby fussed, looking at Pandora like she was crazy, "you could have killed somebody in here."

"Were both of you in this together?" Pandora hissed at Eden, standing up to face them.

"What?" Ruby cocked her head back.

"You looked me in my face and asked me questions about my relationship as if you were so interested and happy about my life, but this entire time you were just trying to make a mockery out of me?" Tears streamed down Pandora's face like a waterfall.

Ruby grabbed her chest. "Anna, you're wrong."

"Why would I do that?" Eden chimed in.

"I knew nothing about this. My happiness for you was genuine," Ruby defended.

"How dare you even *think* I would do something like that," pearl shaped tears rolled down Eden's cheeks. "I have dated this man since I was a freshman in *college*. I was in love with him to the point where I put my future on pause to have his baby. The day of my baby shower, the one you were getting ready to shoot up, I find out it's all one big lie." Eden screamed. That was all she could do at that point.

Tears welled up behind Pandora's eyelids. She blinked slowly, locking her guilty gaze on her best friend. Immediately, she felt horrible.

"This day is supposed to be about *me,*" Eden carried on, "this is my first baby. This is my life. Whatever the heck is going on here with him, *you* can get out of it," she pointed to Pandora, "you can give back your ring...I can't give back a baby."

"I need to talk to Quinn," Pandora paced back and forth. Pulling out her cellphone, she dialed Quinn's number.

"Quinn," she yelled into the phone before Quinn finished saying hello, "I need you. *We* need you."

"What's wrong?" Quinn asked, concerned. She was on her way to the shower.

"You'll never believe what just happened," she spoke hysterically, "I hosted Eden's baby shower today, and I finally met Christopher, but Christopher is Jackson and,"

"Anna," Quinn cut her off, "Calm down, I can't understand you, honey. Speak slower."

"I'm sorry, my mind is going a million miles per minute, and I can't believe this is happening. It seems unreal," Pandora fanned herself.

"What seems unreal? *What's* going on?" Quinn demanded, impatiently.

"Give me the phone please," Ruby took the phone from Pandora, annoyed.

"Quinn, this is Ruby."

"Hi, Miss Ruby. What's happening over there?" Quinn asked.

"Pandora and Eden have apparently been dating the same guy this whole time," Ruby replied. Quinn paused for a second to be sure she heard correctly.

"What?"

"We're all shocked and confused," Ruby replied, continuing to fill Quinn in on what happened. Pandora looked over at Eden, noticing all the color beginning to drain from her face. In seconds, she was pale.

"Eden, are you alright?" Pandora asked, concerned. Eden was teetering back and forth, sweating profusely, and her eyes started retreating to the back of her head.

"Eden!" Pandora hollered. She rushed over to her, but it was too late. "Oh my gosh, Miss Ruby!" Pandora shouted. Ruby turned, just in time to see Eden crashing into the floor.

"EDEN!" Ruby dropped the phone, just as her daughter fainted.

Chapter 8

Pandora stood in the emergency room waiting area of the University of Virginia Hospital, pacing back and forth like a caged tiger. She tried sitting down but popped right back up like popcorn. She felt the need to move, almost without end. If her limbs were moving, the anxiety was gone, or at least she could ignore it for a while. Minutes later, Quinn came bolting through the emergency room door. As soon as she spotted Pandora, she quickly ran over to her, her pink heels clicking loudly against the floor.

"I drove down I-95 like I was auditioning for a role in Fast and Furious," Quinn huffed, catching her breath as she reached out to embrace Pandora.

"Eden's fine. The doctors think she just had a panic attack," Pandora replied. Quinn blew a sigh of relief. "They're checking her out and making sure the baby is okay. Miss Ruby is back there with her."

"Thank goodness," Quinn rubbed a hand down her flushed face. "Are *you* alright?"

"No," Pandora shook her head as they both sat in the waiting room chairs. "I need understanding first, and closure second. This feels like a dream."

"Some chapters in our lives will end without closure," Quinn held Pandora's hand, "I don't think you're in the right frame of mind to go digging for answers right now."

"Like hell I am." Pandora huffed, "I need to process what's happening. It's my job. I need to analyze this."

"No. You *need* to just sit here and relax." She turned to face Pandora in the chair. "You were gonna shoot up a community center?"

"No," Pandora pursed her lips, "I was gonna shoot Jackson."

"Anna," Quinn studied her in disbelief. "You could've killed someone. What if the police would have shown up? What if someone caught you on camera and plastered you all over social media? I don't know anyone in the DA's office better than you, that can get you out of prison and clear your record. You just risked your entire career, and your freedom, over a man."

"He's not just a man," Pandora fussed, "maybe to you, but not to me. This was my future. Empathize with me, just for a second. What if it were you? Let's pretend you and Andre weren't rolling around in a bed of rose petals, since grade school. What if this was *your* marriage?"

Quinn wiggled uncomfortably in her chair at the sound of *your marriage*. Her insides felt like they were on fire. She could still feel her flesh being turned into an internal punching bag by her husband. The sharp, gut-wrenching pains she experienced felt all too familiar...

Thirteen years ago...

Quinn sat in the back seat of Andre's 1995 black Ford Taurus, staring out the window with her arms folded. Andre drove angrily down the two-lane street, honking his horn at other cars in his way.

"This is ridiculous. Your temper is uncalled for," Quinn shook her head and rolled her eyes.

"Oh, my temper isn't called for? Seriously? That's why you're sitting in the back seat because you can't face me!" He was glaring at her through the rearview mirror.

"No, I'm sitting in the back seat because you're crazy."

"Whatever, Quinn," he roared," I can't wait to get you out of my car."

"You can pull over and I can walk the rest of the way. I don't wanna be in here with you either," she fussed.

"Of course you don't, because you know you're wrong," he shouted, "there's no way for you to justify this to me… None."

"I'm sorry," she screamed at the top of her lungs, "I've said it a million times, what else can I do? You refuse to forgive me. You want to stay angry with me. This is all so stupid."

"No, You knew exactly what you were doing. You're selfish. I don't wanna transfer schools just as much as you don't want me to, but I have a chance to play for a D1 team, and possibly be seen by NFL scouts. My career matters too, my happiness means something! Everything isn't always about you."

"Then go," she hollered, pointing her finger. "You don't have to stay, I should've just gotten the abortion when I first found out, instead of getting excited about having a baby with your stupid self." Tears began to fall from Quinn's face.

"Don't give me those crocodile tears. You knew you were pregnant this whole time, and you kept it from me. You waited until I made the transfer from Virginia State, committed to Texas A&M, packed up my dorm, and found an apartment to tell me you're four months pregnant." His face was so hot with anger, Quinn could almost see steam coming from his ears.

"I'm sorry," she continued, "I found out when you were discussing leaving. We've been together since middle school, and now we're sophomores in college. You think you can just pick up and move to Texas, just like that??" She screamed, punching the back of his seat.

"We've been together all these years, what makes you think me switching schools would change that? I can't live my life around what makes you happy. You're not my wife," Andre shouted, slamming his breaks to prevent hitting the car in front of him. Quinn's eyes were bloodshot from crying as her mouth dropped open. She gripped the handle on his back door just as Andre's car came to a stop.

"Let me out of this car, now," she fussed, pulling on the door handle wildly. "I hate you, you hear me? I hope I never see you again."

"Well you have no choice. You're pregnant with my baby and I'm not going anywhere. I turned down the offer," he shouted back, pulling the car over along the shoulder of the highway. Breathing heavily, Andre gripped the steering wheel in anger as veins protruded from his neck. He'd just turned down a great future for Quinn, but he wasn't happy about it

"Well, un-turn it down, you selfish bastard. I hate you," she screamed deliriously. "Go live your life, you're not gonna hold this over my head for the rest of mine. I'm getting an abortion."

"You are not getting an abortion," he clenched his teeth at her nerve.

"I'm getting an abortion," she shouted at the top of her lungs. Andre spun around wildly.

"You are not getting—" His eyes widened, and his mouth opened in fear. Before he could finish his sentence, a big blue minivan came crashing into the back of them at sixty miles per hour. Andre flew forward, his entire body fly-

ing through the front window, landing on the hood of the car. Quinn's body came soaring from the back seat, ejecting through the shattered, front window. Rolling over her boyfriend, her body plummeted off the hood of the car and fell onto the ground. The man in the vehicle jumped out of the car, unhurt.

His eyes bulged out of their sockets as he ran across the highway shoulder. Andre struggled to sit up. A surge of pain shot through his back as his face wrinkled in pain.

"Are you guys okay? I lost control of my truck" the driver yelled frantically. Before Andre could respond, he heard Quinn's loud scream. Her helpless yell was like nails on a chalkboard as she lay on the side of the shoulder holding her stomach.

"Oh My God," Andre yelled. He jumped from the hood and ran beside Quinn, ignoring his own debilitating pain. Dark red blood began to make its way down her legs, while she screamed, writhing in agony.

"Mannequin," Pandora called, breaking Quinn out of her daydream.

"Yeah," Quinn looked around and remembered where she was. At that moment, Eden and her mother approached the waiting room from the back.

"Quinn," Eden hollered. Her face lit up, relieved to see her friend. Quinn got up immediately and rushed over to hug her.

"Are you alright?"

"I'm fine. My blood pressure was through the roof, is all. I need to lay down and take it easy," Eden replied.

"Come over here and sit," Quinn walked Eden over to the waiting room chairs next to Pandora.

"It's so good to see the three of you still so close after all these years," Ruby clenched both of her hands together. Quinn turned around abruptly, with a shocked look on her face.

"I'm so sorry, Miss Ruby. Hello," Quinn gave Ruby a big hug.

"It's okay. It's good to see you," Ruby replied, as they sat down.

"Quinn, this feels surreal," Eden said.

"I can imagine. Why don't you all come to church with me tomorrow?"

Eden and Pandora pinched their faces at her.

"What is *church* going to do?"

"Well, what am *I* gonna do? There's not much I can do to help either of you in this instance. I'm great at my job, but I'm not God. All of my help comes from the Lord, I'm just a mediator. Both of you are in hot water, and you don't need a mediator…you need the source. Anna, you were about two seconds away from being a Defense Attorney, to needing one. You need Jesus, plain and simple."

Ruby and Eden simultaneously broke into laughter.

"It wasn't *that* bad," Pandora shook her head and chuckled. Quinn felt a vibration from her cellphone in her purse. She pulled it out and saw her husband's name on the screen. The thought of seeing his name made her sick.

"Give me one second, let me take this." Getting up, she walked a few feet away from her friends.

"Hello?" There was dead silence on the other end.

"Andre?" She put her ear closer to the phone, stepping further away from everyone so she could hear. The further she walked, the more she could hear a woman's lustful scream in the background.

"Yes, Pastor!" The woman moaned in delight just as the call dropped. Quinn staggered backward, her mind swirling, her breaths shallow.

Eden walked over and approached her, sensing something was wrong.

"Is everything okay?" She asked. Pausing to take in what she'd just heard, Quinn looked at Eden.

"I think I may have to plan a funeral…"

Chapter 9

Andre sat on the white plush carpet, in the meditation room of his six-thousand-square-foot, contemporary home. Panting deeply, he swallowed hard as sweat glistened from his forehead and trickled down his brown skin. Staring lifelessly at the white popcorn ceiling above him, he so desperately wished he could take back the last sixty-eight minutes of his life. Through the dim lighting, he watched Diamond get up from the floor with a satisfied, devious grin. She staggered her perfectly toned, nude body to the other side of the room to retrieve her bra dangling from the porcelain cross hanging on the wall. In that moment, a flash of anger protected him from the pain of realizing he'd failed himself. *He failed his family, too.*

Andre learned in college that the bigger the cosmetic lie, the bigger the whore. From the way Diamond had just performed, she was certainly the mother of them all.

Squeezing his eyes shut, he took a moment to gather his thoughts. In hopes that his wife would be standing there instead, he reopened them to his harsh reality. Andre knew Diamond was trouble the very first time he laid eyes on her. Each Sunday, he preached about healing and deliverance, while judging his members and ministers about their humanity. He was so busy judging others, he left his own closet open and his skeletons were exposed...*again.*

Andre's struggle with lust and forbidden women started long before Diamond ever walked into his church. It began during his freshman year of college. As the son of a well-known pastor, engaging in the usual collegiate activities at Virginia State was off limits. He didn't drink, smoke, party, or join any fraternities. He was faithful to his longtime girlfriend, Quinn, and maintained his spot on the Dean's list for his good grades. That is, until he met Dr. Dandridge, his football coach's wife. She worked at the university as a sociology professor, but she was always around to travel with the team and cheered them on during games. She loved all the boys, but Andre, *he was her favorite*. With him, she'd go the extra mile. From early morning tutoring sessions, to giving him advice when he and Quinn got into arguments, Dr. Dandridge was like a second mother to him. Or, at least, he thought of *her* that way. One particular night, as the football team traveled back to campus from an away game at North Carolina, the devil reared its ugly head. It was late, and everyone on the bus was either asleep or on their way.

No longer willing to tolerate her husband's obnoxious snoring, Dr. Dandridge got up from her seat and headed toward the back of the bus where Andre sat. With his eyes closed, Andre was tuned out to one of his father's audio sermons, on his iPod, when he felt someone flop down on the empty seat next to him. He looked up and removed his headphones.

"Is everything alright, Dr. Dandridge?" he noticed the irritated look on her face.

"You know the one thing that drives me crazy?" she asked him.

Andre shook his head no.

"Your coach's snoring. Just because I'm married to him, doesn't mean I have to be subjected to it," she laughed, "I swear, it gets worse each night."

Andre chuckled. "Be grateful for the minor issues. There are so many marriages on life support in this day and age."

Suddenly, her smile faded, "Yeah...minor," she sighed. "Promise me one thing, Andre. When you and Quinn get married, because you will one day, keep your marriage fresh and exciting. The moment you say "I do", a flame is lit. Don't ever let it burn out and send her looking for love elsewhere."

Before he could agree, Dr. Dandridge inched her hand atop of his, guiding Andre's hand to the edge of her pencil skirt. Andre quickly snatched his hand away, but that didn't stop the Jezebel. Reaching over, she gripped his crotch and groped him into a fever pitch.

As much as he wanted to dislike what she was doing, he couldn't. Eventually, Dr. Dandridge left him alone and went back to her seat, but that night sparked the beginning of an ugly addiction.

Almost every day following that night, Andre would meet up with Dr. Dandridge for tutoring, but the only thing he studied was how to tickle her fancy. Every time he would gaze into Quinn's eyes, he felt terrible for the way he'd been cheating on her, but that didn't stop him. His craving for lust had gotten too overwhelming, and he fulfilled them with no regard for the consequences.

His sexual rendezvous with Dr. Dandridge lasted three months. The two nearly got caught in her home when the coach forgot his playbook and made a U-turn back to his house one day. Andre hid in the bathroom until the coast was clear, but Dr. Dandridge saw that as a sign to end things before they were exposed. He went back to his faithful, dull life with Quinn, who certainly couldn't fulfill his new sexual appetite the way Dr. Dandridge did.

For a short time after, Andre satisfied his lust by purchasing porn, but after a while that wasn't enough either. His unrestrained addiction for lust and vulgarity had become a hard beast to tame.

Obtaining a fake ID with a bogus name was the key that unlocked a hidden world of sex. At least four days out of the week, Andre would sneak into strip clubs, peep shows, and X-rated theaters...he even attended a few swinger parties he caught wind of from one of the bouncers. Andre had become so good at hiding his secret, Quinn, and his parents never found out.

Lust became a very powerful, and gripping spirit in his life. Even when he tried to stay faithful, he couldn't. Once they got married, and he took over his father's church, Andre forced himself to get a grip on his addiction and stay faithful. Over the last nine years, he'd done well. *Until today.*

"So, I was thinking I could cook for you," Diamond grinned, strutting her way over to him, "and then maybe we could go for round two."

Andre jumped up from the floor and grabbed his black robe from the door handle. He shot her a distant, empty gaze, as he tied his robe in a hurry.

"Well, you thought wrong. You have to go- *now.*" Frustrated, he snatched her white satin thong from the floor and tossed it to her.

Diamond shuffled to grab her undergarment before it hit the floor again. With an eyebrow raised, she frowned. "Go? Why? Your wife won't be home until tomorrow. I have an entire night planned for us."

"How could you plan an entire night with me, without knowing whether or not my wife would be here?"

"Oh," Diamond chuckled, putting her underwear on, "you thought my random car trouble in front of your house was an accident?" I knew she wasn't home. She's at the women's retreat at the hotel. I made sure to clarify her wherabouts at the meeting on Tuesday," a grinch-like smile appeared.

Andre shook his head. Now, more than ever, he regretted his decision. Allowing himself to fall victim to her prey was foolish.

"Let me guess, you're gonna threaten me with exposure if I don't offer you money, or some high position in my church?"

"Ministry? she laughed, "I don't want anything to do with your *ministry*. I've always just wanted you, and I will continue to have you when I want you," a wicked grin spread across her face, "or else." Clenching his teeth, he grabbed Diamond by the arm.

"Get out, *now*. I mean it!" Grabbing the black trench coat she came with, he forced her out of the room, down the stairs, and into the kitchen, toward the back door.

"Why are you changing up all of a sudden?" Diamond staggered wildly in her red, six-inch heels. "What's done is done. I don't understand why I have to go."

"This was a mistake, Diamond," he held out her coat, "we'll talk about this later, but right now you can't be here. I need to think."

"What's there to think about?" she huffed, "I gave you what you wanted. This didn't just *happen* by osmosis. I've seen the way you stare at me. You've wanted me for a long, long—"

The sound of the front door slamming shut, startled the both of them. Andre's eyes instantly widened in fear. Chills traveled down his spine, as all the color escaped his complexion and ran to the bottom of his feet.

"Quinn," he gritted.

Diamond snatched her trench coat from his hand, causing her box of condoms to fall out of the pocket and onto the white tiled kitchen floor. She shook the side door handle repeatedly until it opened.

Quinn's keys and heavy purse slammed down on the glass frame of their piano that sat in a room near the front door.

"*Andre!*" she bellowed. Her heels clicked loudly on the hardwood floor as she stormed toward the kitchen. Andre's limbs began to shake, as he shoved Diamond the rest of the way out and tried his best to close the door, quietly.

"Oh *no, no, no,*" Quinn yelled, "don't put her out, let her stay. I'd *love* to meet her," Quinn entered into the kitchen and leaned against the entrance wall. She folded her arms across her chest. With a pounding heart and elevated pulse, she maliciously glared at the back of her husband.

Swallowing hard, Andre locked the door and slowly turned to face his wife. "Hey, Baby," his voice shook. Nervous beads of sweat glistened on his forehead, "I was just taking out the trash…what are you doing back so soon?"

"Oh, really?" Quinn responded, quickly. Her eyes traveled down to the floor and back up at her husband. "Well, your *trash* forgot her condoms."

Andre wiped the sweat from his brow and lowered his eyes to the floor to see Diamond's black condom box by his feet. Looking up from the box, into his wife's eyes, his voice trembled, "Qu- Quinn…I—"

"This is the first time in months that you've actually looked me in my eyes," she cut him off as her tears began to surface. "The first time, Andre…and you *lie* to me?"

"Baby, I don't know what you're talking about."

"Stop it!" She hissed, the tears falling, "I heard her. Your phone pocket dialed me, and I heard her with my own ears."

Andre was speechless. He stood there dumbfounded as his chest heaved up and down, searching for something to say.

"I knew something was wrong," Quinn continued, "you stopped looking at me when you talked to me, you stopped paying attention to me…you gave your phone the attention that I needed."

The pained look on Quinn's face made Andre's knees buckle. His body felt like it would cave in on itself at any moment. "It's not like that—"

"No," she raised her hand to shut him up, "just stop it. There is nothing you can say to me right now, that I'm willing to listen to. You bought another woman into *my* house?"

"Mannequin, I am your pastor and your husband. You're talking crazy."

"Crazy?" Quinn snapped. It was bad enough He'd gone out and cheated on her, but to guilt trip her like she was a fool, just wasn't going to fly. Rushing over to the counter, she grabbed a butcher knife from the knife block and tossed it at his face like a boomerang. "You haven't *seen* crazy yet."

Andre jumped out of the way just in time to see the knife stab itself into the cabinet behind him. He glanced at it in fright, before turning back to face Quinn.

"You are *not* my husband," she screamed, "the man I've known for decades would never speak to me the way you do. He would never disregard my feelings, and make me feel like I'm just an arm charm in his life. My husband protected me. He looked me in the eyes when he told me he loved me, it wasn't just a phrase he used loosely on his way out the door." Storming over to him, she got into his face, and shoved him, "and he certainly wouldn't be caught sneaking a woman out of the back door of our house."

"*I'm sorry*. We can fix this."

"No. *We* can't do anything, anymore," Quinn proclaimed.

"What are you saying?" He blinked rapidly, as she removed her wedding band. Watching her throw it into the sink, he gasped.

The four-carat, colorless, Princess-cut diamond circled the drain opening before dropping down into the garbage disposal. "There isn't a *we*" Quinn confirmed, "it's you, and whomever that *bitch* was that just ran out the back door."

His eyes widened at the sound of her profanity. This was the first time he'd ever heard her curse.

"You don't deserve my love, anymore. I want a divorce." Turning on her feet, Quinn stormed out of the kitchen.

Andre's eyes darkened and filled with tears. The pain of the word "divorce", covered him like a cloak. His legs started to tremble. His initial reaction was to run after her, but he was so stunned, his legs felt as if they'd been cemented to the floor.

"Stay away from me!" she screamed, walking out the door, "you come near me again, and next time the knife won't *miss.*"

Chapter 10
Sunday Morning

As promised, Ruby, Eden, and Pandora drove down I-95 in Pandora's black Mercedes Benz, en route to Tabernacle Church of God in Christ. The recent events at Eden's baby shower left everyone drained and speechless. A word from God was much needed.

Pandora sat in the driver's seat with her tan pencil skirt and satin pink top. Her oversized sunglasses hid the tears that gradually escaped the corners of her eyes each time Jackson crossed her mind. Every so often, she'd use a finger to quickly wipe them away before anyone could notice.

Eden rode in the passenger side with her seat pushed all the way back. The jet-black ankle length sundress she wore, accented her beautiful shape, however, she didn't feel anywhere near beautiful on the inside. She, as well, couldn't get the man she loved off of her mind. Her eyes were visibly puffy from crying all night. No amount of makeup could hide her tired eyes and depressed glow, so she just opted to let it all hang out.

"I'm so not in the mood to go anywhere, considering my life right now," Pandora sighed, "the last thing I want to do is listen to some stupid choir."

"You know, sometimes God allows things to happen in our lives so that we can tap into him," Ruby replied.

Eden rolled her eyes. "Well, maybe Anna has a *thing* that's happening, but I don't. I'm carrying this man's *baby*. God has allowed an entire human being to happen to me. I'm not a stubborn person. He didn't have to go to this extreme to get my attention."

"Well, this is why we're going to church," Ruby rebutted, "everything Quinn said last night was right. You both need to hear from God."

"No, Jackson needs to hear from my thirty-two caliber" Pandora threatened.

"Every time I feel this baby move, it freaks me out now," Eden admitted. "I anticipated an entire life with Christopher and our daughter. I couldn't *wait* to meet her. Now, it all just feels like one big nightmare that I can't wake up from. *I don't want this baby anymore,*" she fought back the urge to burst into tears.

Pandora glanced over at Eden and raised an eyebrow at her honesty, before refocusing on the road.

Ruby rolled her eyes. "I wish you both would stop with the pity party. *Please*. So, you both made a mistake. A big one. Okay, God has given you grace. Maybe you should give yourselves some too."

Silence grew amongst them. Pandora kept her eyes on the road while Eden peered out of the passenger side window.

"I'm sorry to be hard on you'll at a time when I know you're hurting, I just don't want you two to stay in this negative mindset. I don't want you to think that this is the end of the world because of some jerk that played you. You are both royalty in your own rights, and the process of becoming as such, isn't easy. It's the journey that qualifies you to be seated in high places. *This* is a part of your journey. Learn from it. Grow out of it, and be done with it," Ruby narrowed her eyes at them like she meant business. Silence filled the car. They knew she was right. This was just another step in the journey of life. They understood that eventually, this too shall pass. *Today just wasn't it.* Ten minutes later they all pulled up in the parking lot of Tabernacle.

"Quinn told us to meet her in her office," Pandora cut off the ignition as everyone stepped out.

"You guys go ahead and find Quinn," Eden waddled beside them, "I need to stay off my feet, I'm just gonna go in and sit down somewhere until things get started."

"I'm coming with you," Ruby slid her arm under Eden's, "you go ahead, Anna. We'll save you a seat."

"No problem," Pandora replied. She made her way up the ramp of the church, just as a security guard stepped in her path.

"Ma'am, you can't come in on the side," he informed her, "you have to go through the front doors with the rest of the congreg-" he paused for a brief second, recognizing who she was. "Wait a minute, you're that attorney from the Pickett case, aren't you?"

Pandora looked up at the six-foot-eight man and smiled, extending her hand. "Nice to meet you."

"Wow," the guard smiled, accepting her handshake. "You are more beautiful in person than you are on TV. Didn't think that was possible," he stared, star struck by her beauty.

"You're too kind," she giggled. "Thank you."

"Are you in town visiting someone that attends this church?"

"I am, actually. Your First Lady is one of my best friends. Can you point me in the direction of her office?"

"Sure," the guard pointed down the long hallway, "it's straight back to the left. The first door on your right is her office. I just saw Pastor's car pull up on the other side, so she should be in there."

"Thank you so much," Pandora winked. Pulling out her cellphone, she walked past the guard and down the hall, dialing Quinn's number along the way.

Pastors Office...

Andre frantically paced his office floor back and forth, trying not to lose his mind. His bloodshot eyes were red from crying and lack of sleep. He'd called Quinn twenty-seven times that morning, but she didn't answer. Every time he got her voicemail, fear tortured his guts, churning his stomach into tense cramps. Hesitantly, he looked up at the ceiling.

"God, I really messed this up. Please fix it," he begged. Just as he went to say something else, the back door of his office opened.

"Quinn?" Andre sighed in relief, spinning around. His relief was short-lived when Diamond's face emerged, instead of his wife. She was the last person he wanted to see. His heart dropped to his knees at the disappointing sight.

"Are you okay?" Diamond approached him in a skin-tight black dress, and five-inch, pink Prada pumps, "she didn't catch you last night, did she?"

"How did you get in here?" Andre looked at her, annoyed, "you can't just walk into my office."

"Why? Is she here?" Diamond looked around, surveying the area before completely walking in and quietly closing the door.

"No," he said sternly. "She's not here, and *you* can't be here either, Diamond. You have to go."

"You're so tense and angry," she grinned, "I can help you with that."

"I have a service to run," Andre flung his hands into the air, "we are in the house of *God*—"

"So, should we hold off until after service? I can always come back to your house." Stepping back, he did a quick once over of the Devil in Prada that continued to make her way over to him. Suddenly, the five-foot-three seductress that he'd fantasized about didn't seem so appealing anymore. She was pretty good in bed, but other than that she was a pain in the ass. *And he couldn't seem to get rid of her.*

"What's done is done," Diamond placed a hand on her curvy hip. "You've already stepped over the threshold so there's no need to turn back now," she smirked, "you think it's that easy to get rid of me?"

Every time Diamond opened her mouth, he got angrier. Her voice was like acid burning, slicing through his skin. His clenched fists were so tight, his knuckles turned ashen white. His teeth gritted in an attempt to remain silent, but the knots forming in his stomach bought him to a harsh realization: an hour and some change with the church whore may have just cost him more than he could afford.

He took a deep breath. *"Diamond."*

"Unless you're about to tell me to drop to my knees in front of you, you're wasting your breath," she enjoyed taunting him. "As a matter of fact…"

Before Diamond could finish, Andre's temper burst into flames. Gripping her by her neck, he pinned her against the wall. Diamond's eyes widened in fear as she choked and gagged, trying to pry his fingers away from her neck.

"What we did last night was a huge mistake, and it will never happen again," he pointed his stubby finger in her face. The demented look in his eyes let Diamond know he meant business. "If you mutter a word of this to *anyone*, I will destroy every bit of- "

Just then, Pandora opened the office door with a smile plastered across her face. Her smile quickly faded when she saw Andre choking a woman against the wall. She blinked her eyes twice, making sure she wasn't hallucinating.

Startled, Andre jumped back. He immediately let go of Diamond. Buckling to her knees, Diamond held her throat and gasped for air.

"Praise the Lord," He fixed his stance and walked over to Pandora.

"Good morning," she replied, uncertain, shooting her eyes between the two. "I thought this was Quinn's office."

Hastily, Andre escorted Pandora back out of his office and closed it behind him. "Her office is next door, but she isn't in. I'm in the middle of administering deliverance to a member," he looked around the empty hallway. "Is there something I can help you with?"

Pandora glanced at his closed office door, and then back at him. "Did the spirit of deliverance cause you to lose your spirit of remembrance?" She raised an eyebrow, tilting her head ever so slightly.

Andre stared at Pandora briefly before his clouded memory returned. Realizing who she was, he jerked his head back and barked a nervous laugh.

"Anna? What a surprise," he tried fixing his disoriented posture. He leaned in to hug her. "I didn't recognize you with your new hair color."

Pandora quickly angled her body away from him, moving back to a safer distance. "I'm sure you didn't," she gave him a fake smile. "Will Quinn be in soon?"

Andre scratched the back of his head, purposely avoiding eye contact with her. "Oh...she's at home. She was feeling a little under the weather this morning, so she skipped out today. Have you spoken to her? Did she know you were coming?"

Pandora quickly evaluated Andre's movements and knew something was wrong. Fleetingly, she stared at him before shaking her head, no.

"I haven't heard from her in a while," she lied. "I was in the area, and figured I'd drop in and say hello."

"Well, it's good to see you. I have to get back to my office, but I'll be sure to let her know you came by."

"That would be great," she replied, "I think I'm going to stay for the service since I'm already here. I'll let you get back to your, uh...d*eliverance*."

Andre nervously chuckled, "Great. God bless you. I'll see you soon."

Pandora slowly turned and headed back up the hallway.

The moment she was out of sight, Andre turned the knob and rushed back into his office.

Under the weather, my behind, Pandora pursed. She dialed Quinn's number from her cellphone, again. It rang three times before going to voicemail. "She knew we were coming here, today. *Something is wrong.*"

Chapter 11

Three days later...

Eden and Pandora sat across the street from Pandora's office building at a local pizza parlor in downtown Richmond. The run-down, outdated place was much too humid to sit inside. Opting to sit in the picnic bench area outside was a lot more tolerable. The day was beautiful, as other locals lingered around the area as well.

"Eww," Eden turned her nose up in disgust, picking a sausage slice off of her pizza. "This is not beef, I asked for beef."

Pandora, swiping through her cellphone, rapidly tapped her foot on the concrete. "I just don't get it."

Eden looked up from her paper plate with a pensive expression, "yeah, I should've just gotten plain."

"Huh?" Pandora looked up at her. "I'm talking about Quinn."

"Oh," Eden replied, feeling silly, "yeah, it's *so* not like her to just disappear off the face of the earth. I mean, what could've possibly happened from Saturday night up until now? I hope she's ok. Like...breathing."

"Something *is* going on. I can feel it. But, I don't think she's dead," Pandora assured. "Andre would've been a completely different man if she was. I caught so many bad vibes from him when I walked into his office on Sunday. This wasn't the Andre I was used to seeing. He was so out of it, he didn't even recognize me."

Eden shook her head, "that woman you said he was with is probably his mistress. I heard about the church folk and how they get down."

"The way he had her choked up didn't look like they had any sexual attraction," Pandora rested her elbow on the table. "I don't know, maybe things have changed over the years, but my presence made him extremely uncomfortable. He was so thrown, he couldn't even look straight at me."

"Wait a minute," Eden grabbed the napkin from the table and wiped the grease from her fingertips, "when we were at the hospital on Saturday, Quinn got a phone call. She flew out the hospital like a bat out of hell, talking about a funeral she had to plan. Maybe someone close to them died and she just doesn't want to talk. And, that would explain Andre's attitude too... right?"

"...Or maybe someone is *about* to die," Pandora mumbled, remembering the scene from Andre's office, "that was not a man in mourning."

"Well, whatever it is, I'm sure she's fine. When she's ready to talk, she'll call," Eden confirmed, taking a bite of her pizza.

Pandora tapped her finger on the table. She was worried about her friend, more than usual. The uneasy feeling inside of her wouldn't allow her to let it go. Maybe it was the lawyer side of her, but she could tell Andre was holding something back, and now she had an itch to find out what it was.

Unexpectedly, ice cold liquid splashed against Pandora's back. She jumped up from the table and turned around. "What the hell?" She realized who it was. "Samantha?"

Eden stood to her feet with widened eyes. She hadn't even noticed anyone walking up on them.

Pandora worked on a high profile case that involved the gruesome murder of Samantha's brother, John. John was robbed, tied up, and burned alive in his home. The evidence they had against the convicted criminal should have put him *under* the jail for the rest of his life, but Pandora got the criminal off on temporary insanity. He was now a free man, and Pandora, a target for a beat down.

"Are you serious?" Pandora hissed, staring down at her wet clothes.

"Oh my Goodness," Samantha replied flatly, "I'm so sorry. I tripped over my own two feet and my drink flew right out of my hands."

Brenda, her acquaintance standing beside her, replied dryly, "lucky for you it wasn't coffee."

Eden's mouth fell open. She looked at Pandora and then back at the women. Quickly, she grabbed a handful of napkins and walked around the table to her friend.

"Wow," Pandora took the napkins from Eden. She had to laugh to keep from strangling her, "that's really mature."

"Come on Sam, we're late getting back to work," Brenda grabbed her friend by the arm, pulling her away from the scene.

Eden stared the women up and down as they walked off. "What was that about?"

"Just two nobodies, mad because I'm good at what I do. It's alright," Pandora assured. She used the napkin to dry the table before sitting down and reaching for her makeup case in her purse. Shaking her head, Eden wiped the few wet spots from Pandora's shirt as best as she could before returning to her seat. "I don't see how someone with a temper like yours can survive in a career like this."

"I used to say the same thing to her all the time," a male's voice interrupted them.

Both Eden and Pandora's face froze when they looked up. Jackson, the source of the chaos, stood in arm's reach of them. Without an invite, he took a seat on the bench next to her.

Pandora's body instantly tensed up.

"Listen, before you both try to kill me, please just let me explain," he started. "This is just as uncomfortable for me as it is for you'll."

"You've got a lot of balls coming here," Eden sourly spoke.

"I was actually on my way to Anna's office to talk to her," he admitted, "I figured that was the safest place to keep me out of the reach of her gun. I had no idea you both would be here together."

"I wish *I* owned a gun," Eden hissed.

Jackson stared back and forth at the beautiful women with a flinty gaze. Instantly, he regretted approaching them. Pandora trained her vacant eyes on a tree nearby, refusing to look at him. From the strong grip she had on her makeup case, it unintentionally crushed in her hands. She felt the rush of tears surfacing. Before they made their way out, Pandora threw her broken mirror in her purse and got up.

"I'm out of here. Eden, maybe you care to listen to him. You *are* having his baby," she stated, coldly, "I'll be in my office when you're done."

Eden jumped up from the table as well. "Anna, don't leave me here. Please," Eden begged, as tears flooded from her face.

"I want to be a father to my daughter," Jackson stood up, "don't take that away from me. I never meant to hurt anyone, I swear." He looked at Eden. His guilt ate away at his insides knowing how much he ruined her life. Getting her pregnant wasn't a part of his plans.

"Eden, I'm sorry I hurt you. You're young, beautiful, and you were something new after my deranged ex-girlfriend. I loved spending time with you, but I honestly didn't have any intention of getting serious."

Eden felt her heart shatter. His honesty was what she'd been praying for, but the message was far from what she expected. More tears flooded her face, as she lowered her head.

"After a few years, I felt like I was just stringing you along. I wanted to end things, but I saw how much you loved me, and I didn't want to hurt you. So, I kept the charade going. I was wrong."

He looked at Pandora, whose hands were clenched into fists. "Anna, when I met you, you were everything I wanted. The sex was welcomed, but it was everything else about you that I fell in love with. I wanted you, *so* badly, but…I didn't know how to do that without hurting Eden," he shrugged. "I tried dating you both until the time was right for me to let Eden go. I picked fights with her and pissed off her mother, I lied about my finances and where I lived… *anything* to create an excuse to be kicked to the curb, but Eden just wasn't that girl. She had faith in my lies, because I was too much of a coward to be honest."

Seeing that he had both of their attention, Jackson tried his luck and took steps toward them to close the gap. "Right after I proposed to Pandora, I planned on ending it with Eden. That's when she found out she was pregnant. I had no idea you two knew each other. I regret that I hurt you ladies, and I promise I will leave you both alone...but, I want to be in my daughter's life. I made a baby and I want to take care of it. Don't take that away from me," he pleaded.

Pandora's anger faded momentarily as she stared into Jackson's eyes. Her brows slowly lifted when she realized he was telling the truth. She could tell that Jackson genuinely loved her, and truth be told, she still had feelings for him. Right now, however, the elements that stood between her and the man she wanted, weren't going away.

Eden reached for Pandora's hand and held it tightly. *She was so hurt.*

"I don't care how honest and truthful you are," Eden snapped, giving Jackson a cold look. "You should've told me the truth years ago. You knew what you were doing. If you didn't love me, you should've let me go so I could've lived my life...You— ruined— my— life, Chris..." she took a deep breath, "Jackson. You ruined my life for your own selfish benefit, and now I have a child to raise in a broken home. You will *never* see her, do you hear me? Not even if you were on your death bed."

Pandora quickly wiped away a tear as she stepped in front of Eden. As they stood face-to-face she could see the pain in her friend's eyes. "Listen," she muttered. Her voice was low and shaky, but still audible enough for Eden to hear, "I'm sorry this is happening, but torturing him by keeping his baby away will only bring you problems in the long run. There is such a shortage of responsible black men in this world. Don't prevent him from loving his daughter just because he doesn't love you. It hurts, I know. But you have to heal, and then try to work it out."

Eden bowed her head. More tears streamed from her face. "This is so unfair," she replied.

Using her two fingers, Pandora gently tilted Eden's chin up. "Look at me," she replied boldly. "Hate him if you want, that's okay, but let him be a father. Work with him. *Please*?" Pandora wiped the tears from Eden's face.

"I don't know if I can," Eden shook her head.

"You can…I've got your back."

After a few moments, Eden slowly nodded her head, yes. A smiled eased on Pandora's face. She spun around to face Jackson with a blank, emotionless stare.

"Christo—" she caught herself, "I mean, Jack— what do I call you?"

"It's Jackson," he quickly answered.

"I'm going to let you two talk," Pandora said, "I have to change my clothes before court in an hour." She gave Eden a hug and then turned in Jackson's direction. "Do what you need to do in order to see your daughter. I just hope you're a better father than you are a real man."

Grabbing her purse, Pandora hastily walked across the crowded intersection.

Jackson stood there with his hands in his pockets, watching her storm off. *He was crushed.* Even though what he did was unforgivable, in his mind there was still a chance he could dig himself out of the hole he was in. He loved Pandora. He had plans to conquer the world with her. He waited for the day he could be himself and stop all of his dipping in and out of her life, but it all blew up in his face. Knowing that he couldn't have her and that she'd probably never speak to him again, hurt him to his core. Scratching the back of his neck, he turned to look at Eden.

She wiped her eyes and sat down at the bench.

Jackson walked over and sat next to her. "So, when's your next appointment…"

Chapter 12

Quinn stood slumped against the bathroom door gazing lifelessly at the tile on the floor... Physically, she had no more energy left. She'd spent the last three days in a hotel suite, crying her eyes out. It had been days since she'd eaten or even had a good rest. Her chest was heavy and her heart ached. Her once radiant, irresistible, stone-colored, grey eyes, now looked like a gathering of storm clouds. All of the kindness and compassion they once carried was gone. Quinn loved her husband more than life itself. He was all she had, and until now, the only person in her life who'd never lied to her...or so she thought.

For the first time in her life, Quinn actually entertained the thought of taking something to ease her pain...just like her mother.

When she was younger, her mother had an affair with a coworker, who turned out to be her biological father. The man Quinn *thought* was her father divorced her mother of seventeen years. That was a turning point for her.

The day of Quinn's high school graduation, her mother shot herself dead in their basement. Quinn was devastated for *years* following that. The spoiled little rich girl who once had everything now had nothing. She shut down her emotions, and wouldn't let anyone else get too close to her, except Andre. His love saved her life. He made her feel like a queen, regardless of where her throne was. He was an oasis of intellect and intimacy. He loved her mind first, her heart second, and her body always. He showed her that trust wasn't just a word, and boyfriend wasn't just a title.

Andre bought out the elegant beast in her beauty, and it was then that she realized she never needed to be saved. She learned to fly by her own wings. All she ever needed was a co-pilot. With him by her side, she grew up and took over the city. She became poetry in a world that was still learning the alphabet. She captivated rooms without speaking. When she got married, she remained independent enough to fly on her own but loyal and humble enough to remember who was really in charge.

Andre made love to her as if he were creating a priceless piece of artwork. His hands played the piano with her spine as they took each other through a host of emotions. When she glided up and down his thickness, her rhythm told a story. She knew her milk did his body good, and he drank every drop. Their heartbeats were *always* in sync. He was her kryptonite. Years later, even after losing themselves in stress, ministry, work, and carrying the burdens of others, they were still those two young lovebirds on fire for love.

Quinn stood up slowly in the compact bathroom, staring at her frail appearance through the mirror above the sink. Her vision began to blur as tears welled in her eyes. She wrecked her brain trying to wrap her mind around her unfaithful husband, and where her marriage went wrong in the last six months. She felt worthless, depressed, and unworthy, but still, there was work that needed to be done. It was time to come out of hiding before anyone got too worried.

Quinn was a mess. The black skirt and white top that she wore for the last few days were badly wrinkled. Her tears ran all of her makeup down her face and onto her collar, and her hair was tangled into a messy bun. The founders of her sorority, Alpha Kappa Alpha, would've turned over in their graves if they were alive to see the way she represented them.

"Quinn, you okay in there?" A male's voice asked from the other side of the door.

"Yes, Joseph," she said, masking the pain in her voice, "I'm fine."

"Okay…Well, I laid out the clothes you asked me to pick up for you," Joseph replied, "I hope I got the right size."

Quinn stood up straight. Blinking away the few tears left, she used her hands to fan them dry. She pinched her lips tightly together to keep them from trembling. "Get it together, Quinn," she coached, "you can do this." She walked over to the door and cracked it open. "Thank you," she whispered with a slight smile.

"Is your headache gone?" He asked, "do you need any aspirin? Water?"

"Huh? Oh…no. I'm good." Quinn had forgotten the story she told him to get him to come.

The story she fed him had everything to do with having a little too much to drink at a friend's birthday celebration and how she ended up with a hangover. She needed someone to bring her clothing but wasn't quite ready to face her friends. Calling her husband, or anyone from the church was completely out of the question. Joseph was the first person who came to her mind. He would for sure do her the favor without hounding her with questions.

After all these years, that handsome little boy from middle school that catered to her every beck and call was now a grown man who was willing to do the same thing. Joseph and Quinn had been friends for years. In his mind, he was always supposed to be the one to put a ring on her finger. Joseph stood about five-foot-eight inches tall. His sun-kissed, soft brown skin had a natural tan. His head full of sandy curls and caramel eyes made the neighborhood girls flock to him like bees to honey. His freckled filled cheeks, soft full lips, and million-dollar smile were the icing on the cake.

Quinn and Joseph also attended the same high school and college. Needless to say, Andre hated his guts.

In the past, Quinn often wondered what Joseph's deep pink lips tasted like. He was the only other guy she'd ever liked and seeing him around all the time kept those memories alive. They remained cordial throughout college, but their friendship slowly dwindled after Quinn and Andre got married. That's when Joseph realized he would never get his chance.

"Thank you again for coming," she said, "I just couldn't call Andre. He wouldn't be too pleased with the First Lady, overdrinking."

"I understand," Joseph replied, "it's no problem at all."

"Could you pass me the clothes? I'm gonna shower and dress in here."

Joseph nodded and walked over to the bed where he laid out a white, knee-length, straight dress. He returned to the bathroom door moments later. "Here you are."

Quinn took the dress and closed the door. Now that she had a clean outfit, the next task was taming the nest on her head.

An hour later, Quinn emerged from the bathroom. "You are a lifesaver," she said to Joseph who sat on the love seat, "I just couldn't walk out in public like that. Lord knows *who* I would have run into. The stories would've hit the local papers by morning."

"Your ministry has really taken off. Co pastoring a megachurch must have its up and downs."

"Indeed it does," Quinn agreed, "doing God's work is always up and down. It's just good to have friends like you to call during the down moments."

The dress fits nicely," he nodded with a smile.

"Yeah," she looked down at her outfit, "it's a bit tight but it'll do for now. How much do I owe you?" she walked over to her purse sitting on the table.

"Don't worry about it," he told her.

Quinn smiled, "you're such a sweetheart."

"I try to be."

Quinn closed her pocketbook and slung it over her shoulder. "Oh shoot, I forgot to have the hotel call me a cab. Hopefully, there's one nearby. I need to get to my office."

"Where's your car?"

Quinn paused, "Oh, um, I rode with someone else here," she lied. "She texted me early this morning to let me know she had to get home, and there was no way I was following her out of this room looking like a hobo," she laughed.

"Well, I can drop you off," he suggested.

"I wouldn't want to take you out of your way, Joseph. You've done enough already."

"It's not a problem," he told her. "I was hoping I could chat with you a bit, anyway. I actually called your office a few days ago. I left you a message."

"That's right…you did," she replied, "I've been really tied up these last couple days. I'm sorry I didn't get back to you sooner."

"It's alright," Joseph nodded. "I just really needed to talk to someone that I can trust."

You and me both, Quinn thought. "Well, then a ride seems like the perfect time. Can you pull the car up while I get my things?"

Joseph stood up, "Sure. I'll be waiting out front."

As soon as the door was closed behind him, Quinn let out a deep sigh. "I can't do this." Standing in the middle of the floor, she closed her eyes and said a quick prayer. Keeping a straight face was hard enough in front of Joseph. How was she supposed to do this with the church? *"Lord, please give me the strength."*

When Quinn stepped off of the elevator in the grand lobby, she spotted Joseph waiting in his car through the glass door. She approached the car and quickly got in.

"Thanks again," she said.

"You're welcome," Joseph smiled as he pulled away from the hotel. "I just have to stop by my house first and pick up something. It's on the way."

"You're the driver," Quinn reached over her shoulder and tugged on the seatbelt, securing it over her body."

"So, what's going on?" Quinn asked, eagerly.

"It's about me and Andrea."

"Okay…"

"I'm about ready to divorce her," he blurted out. "I wish I was better prepared for marriage. Noone ever told me it'd be this rough," he shook his head. "I mean, I trust God, I read my bible, and I…I pray like

102

crazy when things go wrong, but its like he doesn't hear me. "

Joseph sighed in relief.. It was the first time he'd ever admitted that out loud.

"Well, you've come to the wrong person if you think I'm going to agree to a divorce. The flight of the family, *especially* the black family, is one of my greatest concerns. Right now, the divorce rates are at an alarming 53 percent," Quinn shook her head. "The decline of marriage is a social catastrophe, yet it's also one of the most ignored crisis in the world."

"Well, Quinn, I'm not sure how else I can fix this," Joseph sounded frustrated. "I've been praying everyday, and nothing is changing."

"What else are you doing?" She asked.

"What do you mean?"

"Many times, people use prayer as a scapegoat to keep them from actually having to do the work," Quinn replied, "They pray, and then they'll sit and wait for their happily ever after to fall out the sky. It doesn't work like that. Prayer does not cancel out ignorance. It's *good* to pray, but you also need skills, you need knowledge, you need principals, and you have to understand human nature."

Joseph allowed Quinn's words to resonate with him for a while. Finally, he responded with,

"That makes so much sense. You know, I think you and Andre are amazing together. I listen to him sometimes on the word network, and I love the way he re presents God to our generation. Its different, yet relatable, and it's changed the trajectory of my life. It was you two that inspired me to get married in the first place," Joseph smiled. "Over the years, I've watched the way he protects you and looks at you like you're the only woman in the world. And then I see your submissive demeanor, and how you stand beside him at church. You two just had this connection that went far beyond dating. *I wanted tha*t, but after three years, you're right, I don't think I have enough skills and knowledge to maintain my marriage."

Giving Joseph a distant, unfocused smile, she turned her head towards the window before tears flooded out. Discreetly, she used her finger to swipe away a lingering tear and cracked the window to let in the air.

"The first step to fixing a problem is acknowledging that a problem exists. Which you just did. Marriage can be a beautiful thing, but it's also very challenging. Even those that seem the happiest, encounter their share of problems. It's all the more reason to focus less on how green other people's grass is, and more on watering your own. Love looks different for us all."

Joseph rubbed his chin, "but what do you do when you feel like the love has run out? Andrea and I argue nonstop about every little thing. Nothing I do is right, and nothing she does is ever wrong. The biggest issue is her son, David. He's almost ten, and he's beginning to turn into a problem."

Quinn noticed the passion in Joseph's eyes when he mentioned Andrea's son.

"He's starting to challenge my authority, he steals, he's not pushing himself in school…he is just out of hand, and Andrea refuses to let me discipline him."

"Does David's father have a problem with you chastising him?" Quinn asked.

"No, that's the point. His father isn't in his life. He was killed before David was born. I'm the only father figure he has. Overall, these last couple of years have been rough. I'm not happy anymore. You're my last resort before I throw in the towel. Maybe you can counsel her, or you and your husband can counsel us both. I don't know," he shrugged, slightly agitated.

Joseph pulled up alongside the curb in front of his home and put the car in park.

"You have to help me, Quinn," he finished, turning off his engine.

"Well, I can't just force my services on anyone," she replied, "Andrea has to *want* to talk to me. It may be best if you both came, otherwise she may feel attacked, like you're telling her she's the problem and she needs the help. I can't—"

Tap! Tap! Tap!

Startled, Quinn nearly jumped out of her skin when someone knocked on her window. Both she and Joseph looked over.

Joseph opened the door and climbed out. "Hey, Anna," he grinned at his sister, "shouldn't you be at work," he looked at his watch."

Pandora folded her arms across her chest and locked her eyes on Quinn. "I was on my way there, but I needed to talk to you," she never took her eyes off Quinn.

Reaching down, Pandora opened the passenger side door. "Well, this is a surprise. Aren't you going to say hello to your best friend?"

Chapter 13

Andre drove nervously around town in his candy apple red Range Rover in search of his wife's car. He circled her office building, and the church about ten times, before passing through the park where she took her morning run. He even drove past the homes of some of Quinn's clients to see if she was working. *Nothing.* As he came to a red light, he redialed her number for what seemed like the millionth time. It rang once and went to voicemail. He knew Quinn was upset and needed her time, but too many days had gone by without even a text letting him know she was ok. His next impulse was to report her missing, but he hoped it wouldn't amount to that.

Resting his arm on his window panel, he gazed into the red light.

"Baby, where are you?"

Nine years ago…

Andre stood nervously in his father's office at Tabernacle Church of God in Christ, anticipating the start of his wedding ceremony. He'd waited his entire life for his moment, and here it was. Within the next hour, he'd officially be a married man. His hands were tinged with sweat. He was nervous. Incredibly so. His heart ran with legs like a runner. His eyebrows frowned in worry and anxiety.

"Stand up boy, let me see you," his Father, Pastor Bentley's deep baritone voice, emerged, as he walked up to his son. Andre was dressed in an all-white, form-fitted, one button Tuxedo with peak lapels. Moving into him, his father

straightened his white bow tie. *"You seem so nervous, relax,"* he chuckled.

"I am nervous," he admitted. *" I can't believe I actually made it to this point."*

"Embrace it, and enjoy it. Today is the first day of the rest of your life. Marriage is a good thing when you have a good woman...and you have an exceptional one. I'm proud of you," his father stepped back to get a better view of his son.

"What's the big secret to marriage that I should know about? I just want to do everything right, I have big shoes to fill. You and mom have been married for almost thirty years, happily. You'll have excellent communication, you mesh well together and always seem so in love."

"Great sex!" His father confirmed. Andre burst into laughter. "I'm kidding," he chuckled at himself. *"The key to happiness is to continuously extend the gift of forgiveness. Learn each other's love language as well. You are two different people who express love differently. Learn the language of the other person, and speak it back to one another often."*

Andre walked over to his father's compact refrigerator and pulled out a small bottle of water. Timidly, he adjusted the collar of his shirt.

"Part of me feels blessed. The other part is afraid. I love Quinn, you know? I hope I don't mess things up."

"Good," his father nodded. *"Keep loving her just like that...When she's beauty, and beast. Don't ever stop being her backbone. You've got to be the flashlight in her basement of insecurities. Be her hope, even when it hurts you. Cherish her and protect her-"* his father paused. *"Look at me, Andre." Andre turned to face him. "No more messing around with other women, either."*

Andre's eyes widened in shock when his father pulled his card. "What?"

"I wasn't born yesterday," Pastor Bentley folded his arms, *"and I am your Father. I know you better than you know yourself."*

Andre was speechless.

"All your little hidden fun and games stop here," he continued, *"you've got a good woman. She loves you, and she loves the Lord. You do right by her,"* he scolded.

"You have my word,"Andre nodded.

"I mean it. You keep dibbling and dabbling in sin, your deception will eventually catch up to you. And trust me, hell hath no fury like a scorned woman."

"Man's honor," Andre extended his fist to give his father a pound. *"I've done a lot of things I regret, but it's because of you that I'm able to stand here so confidently. I've had a lot of luck on my side, considering all the things that could've gone wrong."*

"That wasn't luck. That was God, looking out for your dumb ass," Pastor Bentley laughed before turning to walk away.*

The car in back of him honked loudly, breaking Andre out of his daydream.

"Drive!" The angry driver shouted, startling him. Andre quickly pressed his foot on the gas to continue his search for Quinn, silently begging God to extend him grace, and look out for him one more time

****

Pandora stood in the middle of the sidewalk waiting for Quinn to get out of Joseph's car.

"Hi Anna," Quinn blushed, nervously.

"Don't hey Anna, me. This is where you've been all this time?" She asked, "I've been looking everywhere for you. You had me worried sick."

"Join the club," Joseph intervened as he walked around the car. "It took me three days to hunt her down. She's going to talk to Andrea for me, and hopefully help put us back on the right path."

"Oh, is that right?" Pandora turned to look at Joseph and then back at Quinn.

"I can try," Quinn answered.

Joseph's cellphone rang. He reached into his pocket and pulled it out. "Ladies, give me a minute. I have to take this," he rushed up his driveway and into his house. Pandora crossed her arms and raised an eyebrow at Quinn.

"I know what you're gonna say," Quinn started.

"You could've at least called one of us," Pandora dropped her hands to her side, "we came to church like you asked on Sunday. Andre told me you were sick," she gave Quinn a brief stare down. "You don't look sick to me."

Chills flowed through Quinn's body at the mention of Andre's name. "I wasn't sick, I had an emergency with a client, and I got tied up," she lied, "can I make it up to you over lunch?"

Joseph came rushing back out of the house. "Quinn, I have an emergency to handle. We have to go so I can hurry and drop you off."

"Is everything alright?" She sensed his urgency.

"Something happened at work," he explained, "I have to get there."

"Well, she can ride with me," Pandora offered.

"Yeah," Quinn agreed, "go handle your business. We'll set up a counseling session later on."

"Thanks, ladies," Joseph climbed back into his car.

"Come on," Pandora locked her arm with Quinn's, "I could really use that lunch now." She held out her car keys. "And you drive...I need to sit with myself for a few minutes."

Quinn took the keys from her hand,

"Sure. How are you? And Eden? Are you guys better?" Quinn asked as they walked up the street to Pandora's car.

"No. Goodness, no," Pandora fussed, instantly annoyed. "You know that bastard had the nerve to approach us both while we were out in public?" Pandora opened the passenger door.

Quinn paused to stare at her. "Don't tell me you..."

"No, I didn't pull out my gun," Pandora replied.

Quinn opened the back door, tossing her purse on the back seat before joining Pandora in the front. "So...he's still alive?" Quinn muttered, giving Pandora a side-eye as she started her car and pulled out of the parking spot.

"For now..." Pandora grimaced, "but Eden is hurt, and that hurts me to my heart."

"And how do *you* feel?" Quinn asked softly, turning the corner.

"What do you mean how do I feel?" Pandora sneered. "I want to kill him. I'm angry. I'm pissed. I want him to pay."

Quinn shot her a dismissive glance, "do you need a minute to get rid of that angry defense mechanism, and tell me how you *really* feel?" Pandora's nostrils flared. She hated that Quinn knew so much. After a brief silence, Pandora opened her mouth to speak, but hesitation nipped her tongue.

"I'm listening," Quinn proclaimed.

Pandora sighed. "Is it wrong for me to still want to be with him, even if I know it will hurt Eden? I love her, but I also love him. I've done so many hard things in my career that I regret. Every day, I successfully defend clients that I *know* are guilty. Drug lords, assassins, child molesters and rapists walk free because of me, and that doesn't bother me as much as it probably should." Her voice shook, "but this, this *hurts*."

Quinn drove in silence, allowing Pandora to unpack her emotions. What Pandora didn't know was that she, as well, faced a hurt piece. Hiding out from her husband only spared her a few days of peace, but it didn't erase her reality. The scars her marriage created were indeed real. Hearing him pleasing another woman was like a bad tune embedded in her mind. It replayed over and over until she had each lyric down pat. Preoccupied with her own living nightmare, Quinn didn't hear the rest of Pandora's words. Her foot pressed slightly harder on the gas pedal as she maneuvered through traffic.

Andre pulled into a Hess gas station the moment his fuel light came on. He'd been driving around all morning and didn't even realize how fast his tank went. Climbing out of the car, he walked around to the gas pump. As he waited for his tank to fill up, he leisurely looked around. Bone Fish, Quinn's favorite restaurant, was located directly across the street. Memories of endless date nights there crossed his mind. Maybe she was in there...

"Excuse me," he called for the young scrawny gas station attendant working nearby. "Could you get my windows?"

"Sure," the guy answered, "I'll be with you as soon as I'm done."

Andre nodded as he replaced the pump back on its holder. Figuring he had a few minutes before his windows would be washed, he decided to run over to the Bone Fish Restaurant. He knew it was a long shot for his wife to be in there, but in his desperate time, it didn't hurt to look.

Just as he reached the curb, he looked back at his truck one more time before stepping into the street.

BOOM!

In the blink of an eye, a car traveling well over the legal speed limit rammed directly into him. His body rolled onto the hood and slammed into the windshield, causing it to crack. The car came to a screeching halt, as his body slumped onto the ground like a sack of potatoes....

Pandora clutched her face and screamed in terror, but her cries fell upon deaf ears. The only thing Quinn heard was a loud buzzing in her ears as she sat in the driver's seat gripping the steering wheel. She glowered, her chest heaving up and down, staring at her husband's body lying on the ground. When she and Pandora neared the Bone Fish Restaurant for their lunch date, Quinn spotted Andre crossing the street. Rage built up inside her like deep water currents, and without the thought of consequence, she unleashed it. Pedestrians quickly filled the sidewalks, staring at the chaotic scene. The crash also caused the traffic in both lanes to stop.

"Oh my goodness…that was your husband," Pandora confirmed in a panic, "you just hit your husband!" Quinn took deep, rasping breaths, watching the man she loved roll over in agony. Pandora fanned herself wildly with both of her hands. "Oh my God, oh my God," she repeated, attempting to open her door to check on Andre. Before she could get her foot onto the ground, Quinn shifted the gears in reverse and backed the car up.

"Wait...Quinn," Pandora pulled her foot back in the car and shut the door. "What are you doing?"

Quinn didn't answer. She shifted the car back into drive, sped around pedestrians who were beginning to fill the street, and pulled off.

Pandora stared at her friend.

"*Mannequin*... Are you serious?" Pandora's high pitch voice rang through her ears.

Quinn paid her no mind. The paralyzing hurt she felt, spread through her body like icy, liquid metal. Clenching her fists on the steering wheel, she kept driving.

"I don't believe this," Pandora shook her head in a daze.

Panting loudly, Quinn turned down a small street and pulled into an empty parking spot. She put the car in park as the skin around her eyes slowly bunched into a pained stare. Her breathing grew shallow and her eyes filled with tears.

"You *do* know you just committed a second-degree felony." Pandora stated, matter of factly, "reckless driving, attempted manslaughter, attempted murder...in broad daylight. In *my* car." She shook her head, trying to wrap her mind around what had just taken place. Finally, she looked over at Quinn. "What did he do to you to deserve that?"

Quinn stopped the car. Her hands dropped from the steering wheel. Her heart thudded loudly in her chest as she slumped back into her seat. She tried every technique possible to keep herself composed and under control, but she couldn't anymore—especially after seeing him. The breaking of a heart wasn't just a metaphor, it caused actual physical pain. There was a hollow feeling in the pit of Quinn's stomach that made her weak. Her chest hurt, and the dryness in her throat burned every time she swallowed. Her face grew hot and tears rushed to her eyes. She felt like an earthquake had hit. *A really bad one.* The kind where you have to rebuild everything and find the courage to do it. Quinn's face turned bright red as she let out a cry so gut-wrenching, the outburst caused Pandora's heart to stop, momentarily. Clutching her arms to her chest, Pandora froze. Quinn lowered her head onto the steering wheel and sobbed, uncontrollably.

"Quinn, honey," Pandora spoke softly.

"*What* is going on?"

Chapter 14

One week later…

Eden stood on a black step ladder inside of her mother's three-bedroom condominium, adding the finishing touches to her daughter's bedroom.

"You couldn't ask for help?" Ruby entered the room.

"I'm alright, mother," Eden chuckled. Holding onto the handlebar of the ladder, she stepped down and admired her work. "I need to practice doing things on my own anyway, seeing that I'm going to be a single mother.

"You're a single mother with a village," Ruby corrected, "don't forget that."

"I know, and I appreciate it," she nodded. "I'm gonna need it. I applied to grad school for the fall to study business management."

Ruby's face lit up with excitement. "Really?"

"Really," Eden smiled, "I've sent in all my credentials and crossed my fingers. Anna knows a few people on the board, so she pulled some strings to try and get me in. She's actually on her way over to drop off some paperwork for me to fill out."

"Oh, Eden, that makes me so happy!" Ruby rushed over and squeezed her tightly," and Pandora, it's amazing how in all of this, your friendship remained intact."

"Did you expect it to wither and die after fifteen years, over some guy?" Eden looked at Ruby like she was crazy.

"Love is powerful, Eden. I listened to the way she raved about Jackson at your baby shower. He was an entirely different man to her than he was to you. They were engaged to be married. He *loved* her." Eden sat down on a nearby rocking chair and thought about her friend. She'd spent so much time thinking about her own feelings in all this, that she failed to consider how Pandora must feel.

"Hard times will always reveal true friends," Ruby added, just as the bell rang. Ruby walked over and peered through the peephole. Smiling, she opened the door to see Pandora panting and out of breath.

"Eden, you could've informed me that the elevator was broken."

"I didn't know it was broken," Eden looked confused. "It worked fine for me this morning.

"Someone is out of shape," Ruby laughed.

"Tell me about it," Pandora entered. "Quinn runs in the park every day, I think I need to join her."

The mention of Quinn's name sent Ruby's mouth flying open. "Oh my, I meant to ask…how is Pastor Bentley doing since his accident? Did they ever find the fool that hit him?"

Pandora felt a sudden coldness hit her core as she reflected back on last week's event.

"He has a couple of broken ribs and a fractured arm, from what I saw on the news. I haven't spoken to Quinn this week, but I assume she's at home nursing him back to health," she lied.

The day after the accident, Quinn stayed with Pandora for a few days. During that time, Quinn finally opened up, telling Pandora everything. Pandora was shocked and appalled. It was so unlike Andre to be unfaithful. She was crushed for Quinn, and angry at Andre for putting her through this. He deserved everything he got.

"The police don't have any leads yet, but the video went viral on all the social media outlets," Eden stated, "some people said it was a woman driving the car. It's a shame someone could hit a pastor and keep going."

"It's alright," Ruby proclaimed in disgust, "God doesn't like ugly. You reap what you sew."

"Oh yes you do," Pandora spat with a smirk. "Anyway, I was halfway up here and realized I forgot the papers in my car, so I'm going home," she laughed, "I will not walk back up ten flights.

Ruby and Eden laughed

"You came all the way up here just to tell us you'll see us later?" Eden asked.

"If the elevator works, I'll be back in a minute. If it doesn't…see you next week," Pandora laughed and left the condo.

As she made her way down the hall, her phone vibrated in her purse. Pulling it out and accepted the call.

"Joanna Wilson," she said, politely. "Oh, hello Mr. Washington, I spoke to your lawyer the other day, and planned on calling you to set up an appointment as soon as I got back to my office."

Walking up to the elevator, she pressed the button and was relieved to see the downward arrow light up.

"Sure. I'll give you a call back before the day is out. No problem. Talk to you soon." She ended the call and put her phone back into in her purse just as the elevator door opened. She proceeded to walk inside but collided with someone getting off.

"I'm sor—" Pandora ran right into Jackson, who was now face-to-face with her. It was the closest they'd been in a while.

"Anna," his eyebrows raised.

She gasped, immediately stepping back. Nervously looking away, she replied, "excuse me," before moving around him and quickly getting on the elevator.

"It's nice to see you," Jackson followed her with his eyes.

He wanted so badly for her to say something... anything, but she refused. She stared down at the elevator buttons and ignored him, rapidly pressing for the first floor.

Backing out of the elevator, Jackson looked embarrassed, and crushed. Even though Pandora refused to look at him, he couldn't take his eyes off of her. Her beauty was a work of art that he wished he could hang on the walls of his heart. He'd originally come over to return all of the money Ruby spent on the baby furniture, but now he felt directionless— unsure if he was coming or going.

Lowering his head, he slowly turned away. Just as the elevator door began to shut, Jackson spun back around and stopped it from closing. He had so much to say to the woman of his dreams, and he needed to get it out. He wasn't sure what would happen, but he owed it to himself to give it one last try.

Pandora's small frame pressed against the wall, as she wiped away the onset of tears from her eyes. Jackson's presence was a reminder of the man she loved, and the sting of betrayal. Catching wind of her tears, he hurried into the elevator.

"Stay away from me," she darted, angrily, her hand stretched out in front of her.

"We need to talk," he ignored her demand.

Pandora stepped to the side, attempting to pass him, but Jackson used his body to block her path.

"Get out of my way before I shoot you," she hissed, "and *this* time, theres nobody here to stop me."

Jackson wasn't budging...not this time. "Please, stop fighting me and just listen."

"Nothing you have to say is worth listening to," she scolded, trying to push him away.

"I miss you, Anna," he softly lifted her chin to face him, "I can't sleep, I can't ea—"

Yanking away from his touch, she slapped his hand away. Jackson snatched her hands and pinned them to the elevator wall above her head.

"Stop. Stop being so mad and let me say what I need to say!"

"Get off of me!" She scolded, finally looking up at him. His eyes bore into hers with such intensity, her anger melted away like candle wax.

"I never meant to hurt you," he continued, "I meant to lie, I meant to manipulate, but it was all to be with you in the end. I'm sorry this is happening, but I will go crazy if you continue to hate me."

His dominate stare sucked her in like a vacuum. She *wanted* to hate Jackson for everything he'd caused, and she had every right. He wrecked her best friend's life and made a fool out of her own love, but as they stood toe-to-toe sharing a moment in the moving elevator, her heart wouldn't allow her to.

Releasing his grip, Jackson reached over to the panel of buttons and hit emergency stop button. The elevator to come to a halt.

He faced his ex-lover, staring at her intensely. Pandora wanted to protest, but locking eyes with him took her strength away. Her pulse began to race, as butterfly's swarmed around in her stomach.

Moving into her, Jackson pressed his lips against hers. The familiar touch of love sent electricity running through her veins. He wrapped his hands around her waist and pulled her into him, catching wind of her Clive Christian perfume. It drove him crazy. Nothing was more arousing than her scent in his arms. Her lips were so soft beneath his as she slowly opened them, allowing his tongue to creep inside. *That was the flare that set fire to every nerve.*

Pandora's eyes slowly widened, remembering where she was. She couldn't do this to Eden, not in her own home. She was a loyal friend, and this was betrayal in its purest form. Her mind begged her stop, but as Jackson reached down and massaged her neck with his lips, she couldn't do anything but clutch his waist and hope she didn't fall.

"Wait," she panted, finally pushing him away, "we have to stop. I can't do this."

Jackson looked up. "Why would I stop if it makes you feel good?" He kissed her again until his passion consumed her thoughts, and her inner protests were silenced. The more he aroused her, the more she wanted to be touched. The intense, earth-shattering promiscuity in the small elevator came crashing to a halt as they both reached the point of no return, tearing away from their kiss. They took what they wanted, ravenously, passionately, leaving no stone left unturned. Ten minutes later, Pandora found herself quickly buttoning her blouse, and adjusting her skirt. Her seven minutes in heaven had worn off, and the reality of where she was, and what she just did, settled in.

"I have to go," she adjusted her collar, "I told Eden I'd come back up to help her, but I think your presence is more important at this point. I'll call her later."

"Let's go to dinner tonight and talk," Jackson suggested, "we can find a way to fix th-"

"No-no," she proclaimed, finally looking up at him. "We can't do dinner, we can't talk, and we can't do...*this*... anymore, ever. This was a mistake," she reached past him and released the emergency button on the elevator, as it started back up and made its way to the ground floor.

"Our love is a mistake?" he asked innocently.

"Yes...no,...I mean..." Pandora grew silent for a second, trying to gather her thoughts. "I've forgiven you so many times in the past for your mistakes. I felt like a fool in love, but I was content with that. We were flawed, but it made me feel human," her heart sank. "I would do anything to make us work," she swallowed taking a step back, "but I won't do this."

Jackson lowered his head and stuck his hands in his pockets.

Pandora walked over to him and lifted his face up to meet hers. "My career forces me to be cold-hearted and emotionless at times, but when I leave my office and go home, I'm just a regular woman. I have a heart," she patted her chest. "I have feelings, Jackson. I'm a good person, and I have good friends. Eden is one them."

"But what about me? What about love?" He grimaced, "What about Puerto Rico? Everything is set for our wedding. We're supposed to leave tomorrow. I didn't flake this time."

Pandora's heart fluttered and shattered thinking about what could've been just as the elevator reached the ground floor.

"Will we ever have our chance?" He asked.

Pandora shrugged. "Maybe in the next lifetime," she muttered. The door slid open. "Goodbye, Jackson."

Chapter 15

Quinn stood by the large window of her office with her arms folded, staring out into the sky. She thought about her life, and the disaster it had amounted to. She thought about her home, and how she never wanted to step foot inside of it again. Another woman had desecrated it and ruined all of the beautiful memories she held near and dear to her heart. Quinn warred with her mind for days at a time, trying to figure out the reason for her husband's infidelity. Was he not happy? Was he not attracted to her anymore? Was she not attentive enough? Whatever it was, she was willing to fix it. The angry, scornful woman lying dormant felt good for hitting him with a car. The kindhearted, humble wife on the surface, however, felt horrible about it. Andre *knew* it was her that hit him, yet, he continued to text and call her. He begged for her forgiveness and pleaded for her to come home. There was a part of her that wanted to speak to him. He held the truth. The other part of her needed time to get herself together to be able *to handle* the truth. As she stood by the window pondering, a soft knock sounded at the door. Quickly, she turned around.

"Come in," she instructed.

Andrea slowly crept inside. A warm smile spread across Quinn's face as she walked over to greet her.

"Hi Dr. Bentley," Andrea said innocently, accepting her handshake.

"Hi," Quinn beamed, "how are you?"

"I've had better days, but I'm doing alright," Andrea responded. She walked over to Quinn's long, white sofa and sat down. Looking around, she nervously gripped her purse and crossed her legs.

"I've never been to a shrink before," Andrea spoke, "I'm not sure how I feel about this."

"Shrink?" Quinn giggled, walking over to the couch and sat beside her.

"Well, yeah," Andrea nodded. "A shrink. A person who tries to get into my head and tell me how to fix my life."

"Well first off, a shrink is a slang term for a mental health professional who has the ability to prescribe medications that *shrink* your problems," Quinn corrected, "they're often referred to as Psychiatrists. I am not a medical doctor. I cannot diagnose your level of crazy. What I am, is a woman, just like you. I am a wife, a friend, and I'm flawed…just like you. I'm not perfect, but my degree and experience equip me to help you, if you allow me to," she smiled.

Quinn's smile instantly made Andrea feel comfortable and welcome. "Thankyou. I need all the help I can get at this point. My marriage is on the verge of divorce. Joe and I can't seem to get it together. Work, stress, and parenting have us so busy, we don't have time to do much of anything except see each other in passing, and argue. Have you ever been there?"

Quinn nodded in agreement. "Absolutely. Marriage is a journey. It is a continuous, perpetual state of transition that moves from season to season. There are happy seasons, emotional seasons, and seasons of despair…"

"Well, then my marriage has been in a season of despair for almost a year, and I'm not sure how much more of it I can take," Andrea huffed, "my husband is so immature. I'm not sure how well you two know each other, but he's like another child to raise at times."

"I'm not really familiar with his deep-rooted issues," Quinn admitted, "he's just always been a good friend."

"I blame his parents. They both spoiled him growing up. They gave him everything and taught him *nothing*. When Joe and I first met, he was so oblivious about love. I was able to show him how to love me, because he was willing to learn. He didn't mind being taught, *then*. Now, he resents me for it. He thinks i'm dominant, controlling, and a know-it-all," Andrea shook her head. "He argues that I don't allow him to be a man, and honestly, I don't. I don't trust him to be the man I need him to be. I don't have enough faith in him to lead me and to lead my son. I'm sorry if that makes me sound harsh, but it's how I feel."

Quinn looked on with a straight face, masking how she really felt. She had no idea Joseph was one of *those* types of men.

"No, it's not harsh. It's honest, I understand," she said softly.

Andrea sat up and continued. "But I don't always want to feel like I *have* to be in control. I would much rather he take the lead. As a woman, I want to feel protected and guided, but I just don't trust him to do it the way I want him to- but I'm not controlling," she laughed.

Quinn slowly raised her eyes and chuckled.

"Great, you probably think I'm this evil, whack-of-a-wife now," Andrea replied.

"Not at all. Listen, there are two souls inside of us as women. *One mother. One wife*. Both givers, both protectors, and both *dying* to be set free. It's our nature," she gestured. "The problem is, they both appear around the same time, and some men you encounter will need one, just as bad as the other. You should be very careful, however, as to which one you allow in your relationship, especially your marriage," Quinn said. "When you don't know how to separate the two, you'll start to treat your husband like he's your son. The wife in you will make love to him, and the mother in you will try to raise him like he's your own."

Andrea looked at Quinn as she spoke, pressing her hand to her cheek. "*Yes*, that's exactly what's going on. How do I stop it?"

"Do you believe in God?" Quinn asked.

"Of course," Andrea responded quickly, slightly shocked that Quinn asked her that, "my marriage is built on his promises."

"Good. Trust the process and the man that he placed in your life. Joseph may not move as quickly as you would like or love you in a way that you can control, but trust what God is saying to you in those times of frustration. Maybe he's trying to teach you to trust him a little bit more, or maybe he's trying to show you that you can't control everything, and that you need to be okay with that."

"It's just so hard," Andrea winced.

"Well, then the issue becomes *why*? Why is it so hard? Why do you feel the need to control? What are you hiding?"

Andrea's eyes grew wide. Almost immediately, she got uncomfortable.

"Lady, you're really good. You are pulling my card, and I'm not sure if I like it," she laughed nervously, looking around the room.

Quinn folded her hands in her lap and sat back, patiently waiting for Andrea's response. "It's my son."

"Okay..."

"Well, I lied..."

"About what?"

"Joseph thinks my son's father is dead."

"Oh..." Quinn was caught off guard by her statement. "Does your son know his father isn't dead?"

"No, he doesn't," Andrea shook her head, "and he's lived with this story his entire life." Tears welled up in her eyes. "It eats me alive every-single-day."

Reaching over, Quinn grabbed her tissue box from her desk and handed it to Andrea.

"Why start that rumor in the first place?"

Andrea sighed, "I fell in love with the wrong man. He wanted nothing more to do with me when he found out I was pregnant. He gave me money to get an abortion, but I couldn't go through with it, so...I lied. I told him I got the abortion, and I moved away and raised my son on my own. I accepted a job offer here, so we ended up coming back. As soon as I started my new job, I met Joe. This was a secret I thought I'd take to my grave, but recently..."

"Go on." Quinn said.

"David has been asking questions. He wants to know how his father died and when...I never planned on giving that much detail about it. He asked Joseph about it as well. I've always just gotten away with saying I'd rather not talk about it, but I can't keep that up forever."

Quinn sat quietly and listened.

"What do I do? Dr. Bentley, I can't let the most important men in my life find out I've been *lying* to them all this time. In a perfect world, I want my son to know his real father, and I want my husband to understand my logic behind it all. I want them both to forgive me and I want to move forward. *But we don't live in a perfect world*, and heck, I wouldn't even know where to begin looking for some old flame," she sniffed.

"No, we do not live in a perfect world," Quinn replied, "but, holding on to something like this is wrecking you as a woman. It's ruining how you love your husband, and if refusing to stop controlling your husband won't ruin your marriage, the tangled web of deceit you've weaved will *certainly* do the trick. The first step to fixing your marriage is fixing your-self. Marriage takes two whole people. And right now, you're not whole, you have some kinks that need to be worked out.

"I want you to go home, and talk to God about everything in the same way you just did with me. When you talk to him, allow him to talk back to you. When he answers you, *trust him*, no matter what the answer may be. And If you feel up to it, I want you and your family to come to church with me on Sunday."

"If Joseph is up for it, sure," Andrea agreed just as her cellphone rang. She looked at it and saw her son's name flashing.

"Oh," she wiped her face, and rushed out of the chair, "I forgot all about my son's football practice. I have to go."

"No problem," Quinn got up from the sofa. "Think about what I said, and if you need to come see me again, just call me."

"I will do that," Andrea paused in her tracks and looked back at Quinn. "Wait a minute, Joe mentioned that your husband was in an accident."

A tightness grew in the back of Quinn's throat, as she slowly nodded. "Yes, he was."

"Is he okay?"

"He's doing better," Quinn said, "he has a few broken bones, but God is a healer. Anyhow," she changed the subject, "church starts at 10, but if you're coming, I'd like to see you and your family around 9:30, so I can pray with you'll."

"That shouldn't be a problem," Andrea hurried to the door and opened it. "Thanks so much for seeing me. I was skeptical coming at first, but I'm so glad I did.."

Quinn smiled gracefully, watching Andrea walk out. As the door closed, her smile faded quickly. Memories of what she'd done to her husband re-surfaced. Walking over to her purse, she retrieved her phone. She looked at the screen and saw fifteen missed calls and thirty text messages from Andre. Shaking her head, she tossed it back into her bag. She knew she couldn't hide out at Pandora's property forever. Eventually, she would have to face him.

Chapter 16

Three days later

Sunday morning...

Eden sat in the back aisle of Babies R Us, finalizing her purchases in the furniture section.

"How much more do I owe again?" She asked, digging in her purse while the clerk looked at his computer screen.

"Seven hundred and twenty-five dollars for the crib and dresser."

"Okay," she responded politely, reaching into her wallet for her credit card, "and what about my changing table?" The clerk looked at his computer screen again.

"When did you purchase that? I don't see it here." Eden looked up from her wallet.

"What do you mean you don't see it? I purchased it when I bought the crib and the dresser. I put a down payment for the entire *set.*"

The clerk looked at his computer screen, confused. "The cream changing table?"

"Yes, the one that goes with the *cream* dresser, and the *cream* crib," she furrowed.

"I don't see how you were allowed to put a down payment on the entire set. The changing table has been discontinued for months now."

Eden pinched her lips together. "How is it discontinued? I was just in here last week to pay on it."

The clerk looked at his computer screen again. "Maybe I'm not looking at the right one."

Eden rolled her eyes and sighed, irritated.

"Can you get me someone that can help me? I don't have all day, I have somewhere to be."

"One second," he continued looking at his screen to figure out her order.

"I don't *have* one second. Look, I am almost nine months pregnant," she fussed, "I am hot, my feet hurt, and I'm hungry. I don't have the time to—" before she could finish, pressure filled her pelvis and a gush of water fell from the bottom of her sundress.

She gasped in shock and looked down at the floor.

The clerk did a double take, as his eyes widened. "Um..." he stood up, peering nervously at her.

"I think my water just broke," Eden said. She tried to stand up, but the pressure pulling at her pelvis forced her back down.

"Do you need me to call an ambulance?" The clerk looked on.

"Unless you know how to deliver a baby, yes," she sassed in pain. The clerk quickly rushed to the back.

Grabbing her belly, Eden reached for her cellphone and dialed Jackson's number.

"Shoot," she yelled when her memory returned to her, "he's not even here...he's in Puerto Rico." Jackson's voicemail came on after the third ring. "Jackson, it's Eden...my water just broke, and I think I'm in labor." She ended the call just as a wave of pain filled her belly. She dialed her mother's number. It rang three times and it went to voicemail, as well. Eden's face glinted with agony. "Come on, mom, where are you?" She dialed her number again and impatiently waited for her voicemail.

"Mom, my water broke inside the store. Answer your *phone."*

She ended the call and dialed Pandora's number, followed by Quinn's. Both of their phones went to voicemail. A surge of pain circled around her belly, as tears of frustration rushed to her face.

"Where *is* everybody!" she shouted.

****

Puerto Rico...

Jackson lay in his hotel room sound asleep. The alert on his phone went off repeatedly, interrupting his peaceful nap. Reaching his hand over to the dresser, he grabbed it and looked at the screen. Seeing that it was Eden, he rubbed his face to fully wake himself up before dialing his voicemail. Suddenly, his body froze and his heart began to race. He eyes widened, as he shot up in the bed.

"Yes!" He yelled excitedly. His excitement quickly transitioned into anxiety when he realized he was a gazillion miles away. He rushed to dial her number back.

"What's going on?" Pandora was awakened by Jackson's big mouth. Rubbing her eyes, she sat straight up in the bed.

"It's Eden. She's in labor!" Jackson replied, "and I'm a million miles away, in another country. I'm going to miss it," he rubbed a hand down his face, anxiously pacing the floor waiting for Eden to answer.

"Eden!" he blurted out the second she answered the phone. Pandora took a deep breath and swallowed hard. Her eyes lowered and her heart began to race, as she stared at the white gold wedding band on her hand.

****

At the church...

Andre limped around his empty church with tears of agony streaming down his face. His body was wrapped in pain from his hit and run, and his heart was shattered because of his missing wife. He wasn't ready to preach a sermon to anyone. He'd made a mess of his life, and wasn't in any position to speak over someone else's. His mind was delirious from a lack of rest, and his stomach growled from not eating well. He missed Quinn. He felt so empty without her. Walking over to the alter he struggled to get down on his knees. Lowering his head, he spoke quietly.

"Lord," he said, "I haven't talked to you in a while. It's ironic because I tell everyone else to come to you in the time of trouble, but now that my trouble has come, I've been too overwhelmed to speak to you," he choked on his words while more tears rushed down his face. "I have some issues that need to be worked out, and I can't do it by myself."

Quinn slowly walked into the sanctuary. She noticed her husband, and opened her mouth to speak, until she realized he was praying. She stopped and stood in the doorway.

"I thought I could ignore them, or pretend like they didn't exist in hopes that they'd go away, but they won't. My demons, my past, and my mistakes have all come back to haunt me. I'm slowly losing my mind, as well as my wife. I've done a lot of things in the past that I've been able to hide from *her*, but never from *you*. The strongholds i've dealt with for years, I thought they were gone, and I thought I'd moved on. I realized too late, that they weren't. Lord, you can take my church, you can have my money, take my car, take my house, but just don't take my wife from me," he pleaded.

Quinn listened attentively.

"I can start another church, I can make more money and I can buy another house, but I can never find another woman like her, *ever*. Even if I could, I wouldn't want a copy. I want the original. Please, fix this." Shaking his head in regret, Andre opened his eyes and struggled to stand up. He felt an arm gently slide underneath his shoulder to help him. Turning around, he was met with Quinn's beautiful face, trying her best to help him up. His eyes nearly bulged out of the sockets. He was excited to see her.

"Quinn!" He quickly turned to hug her. Pain shot through his body, but he didn't care, he fought through it to hold his wife in his arms.

Quinn welcomed his embrace. "Hello."

Andre's face was full of tears. It was rare that he'd ever shed a tear, and it broke Quinn's heart to see him so disheveled. She'd cried so many tears of her own that she didn't have any more to shed, all she could do was stare at her husband and take in the moment.

"Baby, I love you and I'm sorry," he squeezed her tightly, refusing to let go. "I can't do this without you. I messed up, badly, and I have a lot of things that I need to talk to you about. I'm willing to put everything on the table if it means you'll still love me and never leave me alone like this again," he locked eyes with her.

Quinn studied her husband's face in search of understanding. *Put what out on the table?* What else had he done that she didn't know about? His love meant the world to her, and even through the storm of their marriage, staring into his eyes still made her heart flutter. Leaning in, she wrapped her arms around his neck.

"I love you too. I'm hurt, but I love you, and whatever it is, we can get through it with time."

Andre's face lit up like a kid on Christmas morning. He was willing to tell her *everything* and work towards getting the help he needed.

Just then, Andrea and her son, David, walked into the church.

"Good morning," Andrea smiled.

Quinn and Andre turned around.

"Good morning," Quinn greeted, "I'm glad you two made it. Where's Joseph?"

As Andrea and her son approached them, her smile began to fade, and her eyes slowly widened. She stopped in her tracks midway down the aisle.

Quinn looked back at her husband. "Baby, this is Joseph's wife and stepson. I asked them to come this morning so I could pray with them."

Andre stared blankly at their guests.

Andrea's eyes locked on Andre. "We should probably go."

"Go? Why?" Quinn looked back, sensing Andrea's apparent irritation. "Andrea, this is Pastor Bentley, my husband," she introduced.

An awkward silence lingered around them as the tension in the room thickened.

Quinn looked back at her husband, who looked as if he'd seen a ghost.

"Andre?" Quinn called.

"Well then…" Andrea placed her hands on her son's shoulder, "I guess should just come right out and say it."

Quinn looked back.

"Andre, this is David…*your son.*"

Chapter 17

Pandora and Jackson sat in a restaurant in the crowded, Luis Manoz Marin International Airport, in Puerto Rico, awaiting their flight back to Virginia. After discovering the earlier than expected arrival of Jackson and Eden's daughter, Jackson's honeymoon with Pandora was cut short. His foot tapped nervously against the hardwood floors as the adrenaline rushing throughout his body caused his hands to twitch. Getting ready to embark on some of the happiest moments of his life, Jackson felt like the luckiest man alive. It was hard for him to remain composed.

Finally, he was a married man, and he didn't just marry any woman, he married *the* woman. His stressful, nerve-wracking days of games, gimmicks, and living a double life, was over. Joanna Wilson, now, Joanna Ford, was his to freely love, *forever.* Two years ago, Jackson sat in his living room watching a football playoff game when, suddenly, a breaking news flash invaded his television screen. Jeremiah Pickett, a local truck driver, came home one evening to find his wife in bed with the Governor of Virginia. A few days later, Jeremiah followed his wife and the Governor, unnoticed, in his work truck, as they drove on the highway. Jeremiah trailed behind them, watching angrily as the Governor pulled his car over along the shoulder of the highway and proceeded to have sex with Jeremiah's wife a second time.

An irate Jeremiah impulsively stepped on the gas pedal, driving his MAC truck over the Governor's car. He pulverized the vehicle, killing the politician and his cheating wife. The state of Virginia rioted for their beloved Governor, as Pickett was charged with two counts of first-degree murder, and a death sentence in a federal court for murdering a politician. However, Jeremiah hired one of the top defense lawyers in the country, *Pandora*. She was able to get him a slap on the wrist with involuntary manslaughter, and he only served one year in prison.

After the verdict was read, the news cameras flashed on Pandora. Making her way to the podium outside to address the angry press, Pandora glided through the double doors of the courthouse. Her form fitting black dress, and black Louboutin pumps were the perfect accent to her petite, curvy frame. She was bold, optimistic, sexy, and confident. The way she strutted to the platform made Jackson's mouth water. Her smile flickered across the TV screen, and Jackson felt as if she were smiling directly at him. Her dimples were so deep, you'd think they had a treasure buried beneath them.

As she addressed the furious mob, unbothered by their rage, her face brightened up emitting a light glow, while her cinnamon colored eyes sparkled and glinted.

Jackson's mouth fell open. Even though he traveled the country often and had been in the company of many beautiful women, not one of them ever caught his attention like Pandora. She was a goddess, and he had to have her.

After googling her, and stalking the cases she worked on, Jackson finally managed to get a spot on the jury during one of her high-profile trials. He knew all he needed to do was get within her eye's view.

Jackson was dangerously handsome, and most women found him hard to resist. His girlfriend, Eden, just wasn't doing it for him anymore. He was bored with the young, clingy girls drooling over him, he wanted a real woman; *he wanted Pandora.* Now, not only did he have his wife, but he was also elated to welcome his daughter into the world. Jackson, along with his three sisters and four brothers, grew up without a consistent father figure. Their mother was an alcoholic, and always had a host of men running in and out of their house. The men raped his sisters and molested his brothers. Jackson took his baby sister and ran away from his home before they became the next victims. He went to college, ended up with a great career in accounting, and made a better life for himself. When he first found out Eden was pregnant, he was upset that it altered his plans with Pandora, but he was more than willing and extremely anxious to help raise his daughter. If Eden had refused to allow him a spot in their daughter's life the easy way, his plan B would've been to take her to court and fight for his right to be a father. Jackson's daughter would *never* grow up without him. He couldn't wait to meet her and hold her. What would she look like? Would she have his eyes? His nose? Would she cry when he held her for the first time? Jackson's thoughts raced a billion miles per minute as his heart pounded. Glancing up from his fast food, he noticed Pandora's grave expression. She gauntly gazed at the incoming and outgoing airport traffic through the restaurant window.

"What's wrong, sweetheart?" He asked, licking the rice residue from his lips.

"Nothing," she lied, turning to face him with an unfocused stare, "I was just- just daydreaming, is all."

"Are you sure there's nothing on your mind? You've been quiet and distant since you woke up," Jackson replied.

Pandora rubbed her neck and nervously looked down at her feet.

"Talk to me, baby."

Pandora didn't want to talk. It was much too late for talking now. She'd gotten herself into a *big* mess, and there was no way out of it. She tried forcing herself to hate Jackson. She told herself once their relationship was over that she would never be willing to stretch her time, or patience like that again. She peered up at Jackson, who licked his lips and focused his eyes on her, eagerly awaiting a response. The way he stared at her made her muscles tense and her stomach flutter. Aside from being amazing in bed, Jackson also made more money than her and handled his business. Pandora felt protected, loved, and cared for when Jackson was around. She couldn't wait to be his wife, and the wait was finally over, but the feelings that flooded her mind were far from happy. Marriage was ordained by God and was meant to be a blessing, *but she didn't feel blessed.* Pandora felt like the scum of the earth. After their encounter at Ruby's housing complex, Pandora cried the whole way home. She thought she'd never see Jackson again, but he refused to take *no* for an answer. He followed her to her home, begging and pleading for her to reconsider.

"This is fate, Pandora. A love like ours doesn't happen every day," Jackson spoke softly, gripping her waist while he stared into her eyes. "Let's run away and get married. I know this goes against everything you stand for, but sometimes you have to stand up for love, too."

Pandora tore away from his grasp. Tears flooded the cracks of her eyes.

"No," she spoke firmly, "I cannot. I *will* not." She paced her kitchen floor trying to convince herself not to do it. "*Absolutely not.*" But she did it anyway. Pandora allowed an opportunity to control her loyalty, and now her character was in question. Her law degree and fancy methods of manipulation worked well on a Grand Jury but would never fly with her best friends. What would happen now? She thought. Tears welled up in her eyes as she batted her eyelids in an attempt to control them.

"I'm alright, really," she offered a fake chuckle before lifting her fork and taking a bite of her salad.

"The food here is delicious…even at the airport," Jackson took a sip of water from his glass.

"I agree, it's amazing," Pandora nodded through her chewing, turning her head toward the restaurant window. She nearly spit her food across the table when she saw Tracey, a competitor at another law firm walk through the airport doors. Tracey was the biggest nuisance in all of Virginia. If you ever wanted your personal business put on blast, twisted around, and leaked to the press, let Tracey find out about it. Pandora was supposed to be in Maryland working on a murder case that Tracey wanted to take, but the client chose Pandora instead. The last thing she needed was for Tracey the troublemaker to find out she left the country in the middle of a case to get married. Pandora crossed her fingers and prayed to every God on the planet that Tracey was not coming into the restaurant. Much to her dismay, Tracey noticed Pandora through the window, en route to the bathroom next door. Her eyes widened as she paused momentarily to do a double take. She smirked hard before hurrying inside the restaurant. Pandora quickly put her hands into her lap and slid off her wedding band just as Tracey approached their table.

"Well, well, well," Tracey smirked deviously, "what a surprise to see you in Puerto Rico. Shouldn't you be in Maryland working on the Brenner case?" Tracey deliberately raised her eyebrows and crossed her arms, giving Pandora a quick once over.

"I had an urgent family matter to attend to," Pandora lied, sitting up in her chair. "I can't say that I'm surprised to see you here, seeing as I put you out of work. I take it your vacationing?" She winked, arrogantly.

Tracey's smirk quickly faded as she sneered at Pandora. "Whatever, Anna. You competed with me unfairly for that spot," she pointed out, "it's alright though. Enjoy your shine. It won't last forever," she pressed her lips together in a fake smile.

"Honey, I don't compete for spots, I *am* the spot." Pandora spat.

"Whatever," Tracey shook her head. She noticed Jackson across the table and smiled in his direction. "I'm so sorry, how rude of me. I'm Tracey," she stuck her hand out, "and you are?"

Jackson looked up and pleasantly smiled. Putting his fork down, he stuck his hand out to meet hers.

Pandora immediately leaned forward and spoke before he could. "This is Jackson. One of my many associates," Pandora said hastily, giving Jackson a quick eye in hopes that he would play along.

Jackson's face almost cracked and fell on the floor, but he got it together quickly and extended his hand.

"A very handsome associate I might add," Tracey flirted, shaking his hand slowly.

"Thank you," Jackson replied, letting go of her hand, immediately grabbing his fork to go back to his lunch. *He was pissed.* His clenched jaw and grimacing sneer let Pandora know it. He stabbed his fork into his plate, aggressively picking up his food.

"I see you're married," Tracey stared at his ring, "what a lucky woman. She let you come all the way to Puerto Rico without her?" She glanced over at Pandora. "Anna, I hope you're behaving. God knows I wouldn't be." Tracey laughed, obnoxiously as Pandora sat up straight, slightly agitated, and cleared her throat.

"His wife is here. Very close by, might I add, and she is the devil. You'd better watch yourself flirting with her husband. She'll send you back to Maryland in a body bag," Pandora raised an eyebrow, taking a bite of her food. Peering down at her watch, Tracey's smile quickly faded.

"Would you look at the time? I am late for...something," she laughed nervously, peering around. It was nice meeting your acquaintance, Jackson," Tracey spoke hastily as Jackson looked up with a fake wince. "You guys enjoy the rest of your lunch. Pandora, I will cross paths with you in court at some point."

"I'll be waiting," Pandora replied, amused as Tracey quickly turned and left the Restaurant. Pandora adjusted her posture and chuckled, turning to face Jackson. "I swear, she's like Jesus. She's everywhere. What are the odds of running into—"

"One of your many associates?" Jackson bared his teeth, finally releasing his anger, catching Pandora off guard.

"No, of course not," Pandora replied, sharply, "she has one of the biggest mouths in-"

"Where's your wedding band?" Jackson's mouth gaped open, looking down at her ring finger.

"I took it off, momentarily," Pandora proclaimed. Her eyebrows furrowed, annoyed that Jackson cut her off twice. Jackson slung his fork on his plate and slid his chair back.

"What the hell, Anna?" He fussed, "what are you doing? What is this about?"

"Listen, that was one of my biggest competitors. I'm not ready for her to find out yet," Pandora scolded, "I'm not ready for anyone to find out until the time is right."

"I'm confused," Jackson replied sharply. "Until w*hat* time is right? This is about us. Our love. Our life. I'm not walking on eggshells for your stupid friendship and colleagues, this is-"

Pandora slowly widened her eyes and jerked her head back in disgust. "Excuse me?" Locking eyes on Jackson, she flared her nostrils. "There is nothing *stupid* about my friendship with Eden or my career," she bellowed with a snare. "Eden has been my best friend since middle school. We have been there for each other through thick and thin for as long as I can remember. That is my heart," Her voice began to tremble, and her face turned a bright shade of red. "That is a piece of my soul that I just sold for love. She's getting ready to have a baby. I'm supposed to be there for her, but here I am, trying to sneak back into the country with the father of her child who I went and married."

Pandora shook her head in disgust. She still couldn't believe what she did to her friend. "I feel like a horrible person. I have no idea how to explain this to her," tears fell from her eyes, as Jackson looked on in silence, "but I have to at least try. On *my* terms. Not yours," she scolded. "I just threw away fifteen years of friendship…for you," She pointed at him as her voice lost power with each word. "Just give me some time to figure this out."

Jackson felt bad. The Pandora he knew was sassy, cold and ruthless. He didn't think she had any friends, with her attitude. He saw the pain in her eyes, and even though he didn't understand the sacrifice she made for him, he hated to see her cry. He grabbed a napkin from the table and reached over, attempting to wipe her eyes. Pandora rejected his gesture, quickly fanning herself to prevent more tears from forming.

"I'm okay," she forced a laugh, "I'm alright. Just give me some time."

"Flight 586 is now boarding in zone 3. Flight 586," the attendant spoke through the loudspeaker. Jackson slid his wedding band off and put it in his pocket before he stood up.

"Take all the time you need," he muttered.

"Is that us?" She asked.

"Yeah, that's us…" he reached down to pick up his carryon luggage.

"You're not upset with me are you?" Pandora gazed up at him, watching him adjust his blazer.

"Anna, I'm sorry I don't understand your friendship with Eden. She's an ex to me," Jackson shrugged. "You're my wife. I lied, manipulated, and put my character as a man on the line just to get you. Man, I dreamed about the day I could have you forever, and it's finally come. I don't care what anyone thinks of me. I don't care what friends I lose, I'll risk it all to have you next to me at night." His words caused her heart to skip a beat, "but I will give you all the time you need."

Picking up Pandora's carryon bag with his free hand, he turned to exit the restaurant. Pandora reached into her purse and took out a fifty-dollar bill, placing it on the table next to the check. Getting up quickly, she hurried to catch up with Jackson, accidentally leaving her purse behind.

"Thanks for understanding."

They walked through the noisy crowd and proceeded into the line to board their flight.

"On another note, I'm excited to start a life with you," Jackson said excitedly, changing the subject, "North Carolina is a beautiful place to raise a family, and my bachelor pad is just waiting for a female's touch."

Pandora looked at him like he was crazy. Moving to North Carolina was never discussed.

"North Carolina?" She raised her eyebrows.

"Yes, the house I brought you to before, and told you it was my mother's?" He chuckled, "it's mine."

Pandora turned her nose up, disgusted. "Ew, I had more pity when I thought it was your mother's. The outside looks run down and ancient, and the inside is outdated. I'm not moving in there."

"Well, we can fix it up," Jackson said, excited.

"Jackson, my firm is in Virginia, but I'm back and forth between there, and my partner firm in Maryland. I have two properties, one in each state," she replied boisterously, "pick one, and you can move in with me."

"My house has been in my family for over a hundred years," Jackson darted.

"Looks like it," Pandora mumbled under her breath.

Jackson became annoyed. "I'm not giving up my house to move in with you," he fussed, continuing to move ahead in line. "You're *my* wife. How does that look?"

"It looks like your *wife* has the better house and the better location for her job. You travel via airplane all the time, so this doesn't affect you. You can keep your house, just rent it out."

"Pandora, I am not coming to move in with you, *you* will come to live with me. End of story," He pointed sharply, opening his bag to find his boarding pass.

"Baby, I don't care if Noah built an ark in that house and we had to go there to escape the flood. I'd be a drowned bitch before I move my things into that ancient, mummified house," she spat back, pulling out her boarding pass, just as they reached the attendant.

Jackson's eyes widened. He tried everything he could to hold his temper together. Pandora's sassiness used to turn him on, but now it was starting to make him mad.

"Joanna?" The boarding attendant spoke, breaking through their dispute, "wow, it's great to see you again," she smiled.

Pandora looked up from her wallet. "Oh my..." a smile spread across her face. "How are you, Charlotte?" They both reached out and embraced one another.

"I'm wonderful now, thanks to the best lawyer in the world. I owe you my life, girl."

Pandora gave Charlotte a brief stare and a wink.

Charlotte once lived in Virginia with her abusive husband. After being tormented for over twenty years, she butchered him to death. Pandora got her murder charges acquitted, and Charlotte found herself a Spanish husband, before moving out of the country to start a new life.

"I'm so happy for you," Pandora gleamed. "It's great to know you're doing okay."

"Thanks so much. Oh, by the way, the plane is filled to capacity. All of the seating is a bit mixed up, so there's a possibility that you and your....," Charlotte looked up and smiled at Jackson, who's face was fire engine red.

"I'm her pet," Jackson responded angrily as he slipped Charlotte his boarding pass, "nice to meet you."

Pandora's eyes flew open and grew wider than the globe as she jerked her head up at Jackson. Charlotte's mouth slightly opened, watching Jackson swarm past her to board the aircraft. Pandora blushed, trying everything she could not to show her embarrassment. She rubbed the side of her neck and bit her lip.

"I— I'm sorry. He's my client, and he's not having a good morning," she lied, clearing her throat.

"Oh, it's quite alright," Charlotte nodded. "Here is his boarding pass back, and yours. Have a good flight."

"Thank you," Pandora smiled. She walked past Charlotte and high tailed it onto the plane. She glared at Jackson the second she spotted him in the middle of the aisle, putting his carryon bag in the overhead. He could feel her death stare growing closer as she walked toward him with a vengeance, but he paid her no mind. He flung her carryon bag into the seat in front of him and reached into his pocket for his cellphone. Pandora was livid. She hated to be embarrassed. Most of their relationship was spent having sex and missing each other. She had no idea how much of a jerk Jackson could be. Pandora walked into the end row where Jackson placed her bag, leaning over her seat to face him as he slouched down in his chair.

"I am a lawyer!" She declared angrily through gritted teeth, "I have a reputation to protect. *Please* don't embarrass me like that *ever* again," she scolded, folding her arms.

"Who me? Your associate with the old crypt keeper house? How could *I* embarrass *you*?" His eyes glared at her briefly before sliding his headphones on his ears. Jackson turned on his music, ignoring Pandora's presence.

Pandora clutched her chest and gasped, as her ears began to pound. It took every ounce of strength she had not to wrap around his behind like a Black Mamba and squeeze the life out him. No one had ever spoken to her that way and gotten away with it. *Who did he think he was?* She forced herself to turn around and sit in her seat next to the elderly couple that occupied the two chairs next to her. Pandora folded her arms, glaring at the back of the seat in front of her.

"Newlyweds?" The elderly woman sitting next to her asked sweetly, slightly amused by Pandora's angry disposition. Pandora turned, giving the woman a brief stare before nodding her head.

"Yeah," she replied in a low, irritated voice. The woman smiled, touching Pandora's hand.

"Welcome to marriage, honey. Get used to it."

Chapter 18

Quickly blowing out a gasp of air, Quinn turned to face Andrea, and then back at her husband.

"I'm sorry, what?" She forced a chuckle, tilting her head to mentally weigh in on Andrea's words. Swallowing hard, Andre shifted his gaze between Andrea and her son. His heartbeat sounded like a bass drum inside his chest. He closed his eyes, pinching the cracks of them with his two fingers.

"This is not happening right now," he reassured himself. Quinn turned to face him, noticing his disheveled demeanor. Her eyes pierced at him like a pointed gun to its target.

"You *know* her?" Quinn asked in a sharp tone that demanded an immediate response. Indeed, he knew Andrea, but in that moment he wished he didn't. He knew her favorite perfume was Cool Water because she left her scent all over his many hotel rooms when she left for the night. He knew what her insides felt like, and what they tasted like. After listening to her scream and beg in his ear so many times, he had the sound of her voice imbedded in his memory. How could he forget *her?* Eleven years ago, Andre walked along a bike path in a local park, in downtown Virginia. It was 1:30 in the morning, and he had just come back from Paris, France after surprising Quinn with a trip to the Eiffel Tower, where he proposed to her. Andre knew he wanted to marry Quinn after he gave up his dream of playing D1, college football to stay within her reach while she carried their baby. He couldn't stand her spoiled ways, and after being together every day for fifteen years, he sometimes grew annoyed by her company. But there was something about her that he couldn't leave. Her love was an addiction, and the thought of him ever breaking up with her and seeing her with someone else made his skin crawl. It took him three jobs and three years to save up the twenty thousand dollars to buy her the four-carat, colorless diamond, engagement ring she went crazy over every time they walked past the Zale's window. Money burned his pockets. Andre couldn't save a dollar if his life depended on it, but for Quinn, he made it happen. Seeing the look on her face, and the tears that trailed from her eyes as he held out the diamond and professed his love for her was an image he would never forget. As he walked through the park thinking about his next move, a young girl running in front of him accidentally tripped and was on her way into the ground. Andre's mouth flew open and he flung his arms out to catch her before she hit the ground.

"Are you alright?" Andre asked.

"I'm fine. Thank you so much," the girl replied, embarrassed, regaining control of her balance. "I didn't see this big ol' rock in front of me," she laughed, nervously.

Andre noticed her young face and squinted his eyes to get a better look at her.

"Should you be out in the park this late anyway? You look a little young."

"I'm sixteen," she laughed, making note of his handsome face. "You don't look that much older than me, maybe you should go home too."

"I'm twenty-two," Andre stated, "sixteen is too young to be in a park on this side of town, this late," he scolded. "Suppose I was a rapist." The damsel looked him up and down slowly before biting her lip into a grin.

"You can't rape the willing," she flirted. Andre slowly jerked his head back. "I'm Andrea," she smiled.

"Andre," He nodded. Andre promised himself after proposing to Quinn, that he wouldn't cheat on her anymore, no matter how tempting it was. He tried his best not to be turned on by a girl much younger than he was. However, the red moon that shined through the trees gave him a glimmer of Andrea's pecan colored skin, glistening with sweat from her workout. She had the body of a twelfth grade cheerleader but breasts the size of Texas. Her wet tank top stuck to her chest, leaving very little to the imagination. Andre couldn't help but stare.

"You should really get home, Andrea. It was nice meeting you," He stepped back from her in hopes of making a clean getaway. Andrea gave him a seductive stare before boldly using her hand to grip his erection.

"I'm not sure your friend wants me to leave." After being repeatedly raped by her stepfather when she was a little girl, Andrea grew up craving the touch of older men. She was in and out of foster homes since she was eight years old. Everything about her life was inconsistent. However, the way grown men took advantage of her, reminded her of her stepfather. She couldn't stand him, but the touch was so familiar, she began searching for it in anything that looked and smelled like a pervert. After trying to get away from her two more times, Andre gave in to his lust and they gave each other what they both wanted. After biting her forbidden fruit, Andre couldn't leave Andrea alone. He opened up a whole new world of perversion for Andrea, and she was hooked to him like white on rice. His sex became a drug to her, and she couldn't go a day without it. She fell in love with him, and he used it to his advantage. He introduced her to strip clubs, threesomes, and orgies. She did everything he asked of her. In return, Andre funded her shopping sprees, paid for her prom dress, and anything else she desired. Andrea was crazy in love, and Andre was crazy in lust. Their connection worked, until one year later when she popped up pregnant and Andre almost lost his mind. Andrea wanted to start a family and begged him to consider being in a relationship. Andre told her he wasn't ready for love or fatherhood and gave her the money to get an abortion. Andrea was crushed, as Andre began to duck her and ignore her phone calls. She went to the abortion clinic alone, but after seeing the horrible videos of what they did to unborn babies, Andrea couldn't go through with it. She wanted to have Andre's baby, even though he broke her heart. She thought maybe if she had his child and eventually allowed them to meet, he would reconsider his decision and want to be with her. She moved out of the state with her aunt and hid her pregnancy. Once her son was seven years old, she was offered a good job back in Virginia, so she moved back. Upon her arrival, she couldn't find Andre anywhere. He changed his number, deleted his social media networks, and seemed to have vanished. She eventually met Joseph and fell in love. Andrea gave up the search for her son's father and told everyone he had died. Andre was relieved after finding out Andrea had moved out of the state. He assumed she had taken care of her business and left him alone for good. Eleven years later, however, the skeletons in his closet had all come out to play. Rubbing his forehead nervously, Andre looked over at his wife. The pained expression on his face said everything his words couldn't.

"I'm sorry," Andrea hesitated, "I didn't- I had no idea this was your husband," she stuttered. Quinn's breaths begin to quicken, and her eyebrows raised while she shifted her glare toward Andrea just as a Deacon walked into the sanctuary. Andre's knees began to buckle, but he quickly adjusted his posture and fixed his face.

"Good morning Pastor," the deacon said, elated.

"Praise the Lord, Deacon Jones," he responded with a fake smile, limping toward his wife and Andrea. "Ladies, we need to move this into my office." Andre quickly slid his arm under Quinn's, who was unable to alter her facial expression. Her body was stiff and her face looked as if she had seen the devil himself.

"First Lady, how are you this morning?" Deacon Jones asked, attempting to walk over to her as Andre forcefully ushered her away from the Deacon into the direction of his office. He motioned for Andrea to follow.

"Baby, I need you to sit out here for a little while, okay?" Andrea muttered softly to her son, kissing his forehead as he nodded in agreement.

"Deacon, will you start the prayer, and if need be, I'm going to need you to preach. I'll keep you posted," Andre spoke in a shaky voice, opening the door to his office.

"Yes Sir. I'm always ready," The Deacon smiled, "the Lord is constant-"

"Praise God. Thank you," Andre cut him off quickly, allowing Andrea to enter his office before shutting his door. The second the office door closed, Quinn tore away from her husband's arm. Her face turned red, and the blood under her skin began to boil. Her muscles quivered as she moved to a distance where she could see her husband and his former mistress at the same time.

"Somebody better start talking. *Now,*" Quinn stated sharply. Andrea looked at Quinn, and her stomach felt rock hard. Her heart beat so fast, she thought it would give out at any minute. The soft-spoken psychologist she met a couple days prior that looked as if she wouldn't hurt a fly, was gone. The scorned wife standing in front of her looked like a ticking time bomb. The kind that could wipe out an entire city if it wasn't diffused in time.

"Are you sure this is a good time?" Andrea asked hesitantly. "Maybe I should come back another—"

"Why are you here?" Andre blurted out, angrily, "and why is a child that you were paid to abort over ten years ago sitting in my sanctuary?" He fussed coldly.

Seeing the man she once loved for the first time in over ten years, instantly brought back so many beautiful memories for Andrea, but the way he glared at her with so much hostility, wanting to know why she didn't kill their son like she was asked, broke her heart.

"I couldn't do it, Andre," she swallowed hard, "I was going to, but you weren't there to do it with me and I didn't want to go through with it alone, so I moved away and raised him on my own. I'm sorry," tears flowed from her face as she covered her mouth with her hands. Andre's chest heaved up and down in anger as his animalistic stare locked Andrea in place.

"I can't believe you-"

"What is going on!?" Quinn shrieked in anger with a lack of empathy for Andrea's broken heart. She tried hard to hold herself together, but slowly, she was losing it. She used her two fingers to rub her temples as Andrea and Andre snapped their heads in her direction.

"A mistake, Quinn," Andre assured in a low, shaky voice, "a mistake that happened after an argument between you and me over ten years ago." Andrea's eyes squinted as she wiped her tears.

"Wait, excuse me? A mistake that happened during an argument?" Andrea asked, looking at Andre confused. "How long have you two been together?

"That's none of your concern—"

"Since *middle* school," Quinn gritted, cutting Andre off.

Andrea stared at Andre in confusion before opening her mouth in shock. "Wow...The truth finally comes out," she nodded. Quinn turned to face her husband as if she were about to faint.

"Andre, how many times have you cheated on me?" She asked softly, "you had a child with another woman?" She stared into her husband's eyes in horror. Andrea slowly shook her head in disgust, watching Andre attempt to console his wife.

"Cheating is *not* the word to describe this man," she spat, bitterly, crushed at the news of him being in a serious relationship the entire time they were together. Andre spun around to face Andrea.

"Andrea, you need to leave, I'm talking to my wife," he muttered angrily "and your-"

"No, you're *lying* to your wife. Just like you lied to me for over a year," Andrea stated sharply, glaring at Andre. "How dare you make me out to be some groupie that just *happened* during an argument! All the love we made, the orgies, the threesomes. For over a year," Andrea shook her head in disgust. "That doesn't sound like an indiscretion after an argument."

Quinn's eyes gaped open as if the rapture had taken place and she was left behind. She gripped her chest and turned toward Andre to speak, but nothing came out. In that moment, Andre wished a pack of wild Elephants would've stampeded into his office and trampled the hell out of Andrea. He rubbed a hand down his face and all the hair on his neck stood up with each word Andrea spoke. He wanted to tell his wife about his past infidelity himself. *He didn't plan for her to find out like this.*

"Baby, please don't listen to any of this," he spoke softly, walking into his wife's personal space. "She's a whore, there's no telling who that kid belongs to. I highly doubt he belongs to me." Quinn felt the room spin and moved back quickly, holding her head as she stumbled against Andre's desk for support. Her legs felt like Jell-O, and her heart felt like it had been ripped out of her chest. Her nerves danced around in her body as she saw her life begin to flash before her eyes.

"A whore?" Andrea spoke in a high-pitched voice. Andre paid her no mind.

"I want a blood test," Andre said sharply. "Until then, get out of my office so I can talk to my wife. *Please.*" He darted.

"I should've never come here. I should've listened to my gut instinct and stayed home in bed," Andrea said to herself, swinging her purse over her shoulder in a hurry. "Dr. Bentley, I'm sorry." She glanced over at Quinn and felt terrible. Quinn gripped the edge of her husband's desk with one hand, and the side of her face with the other in an attempt to grasp her reality. She looked up at Andrea with a vacant stare as Andrea's eyes filled with tears. "I'm so, so sorry, I-" Andre's side door slowly crept open, startling him. His soul nearly jumped out of his body and banged on the door of hell when he spun around to see Diamond creeping her way in with her back facing them.

"We need to talk," Diamond said with an attitude, "and I don't care about your wife's whereabouts, or if she's on her way here," Diamond pranced around to face him with one hand on her hip. "If you ever put your hands on me—" she stopped in her tracks when she noticed two other women in the room facing her, Quinn being one of them. Diamond immediately jerked back. Quinn's mouth propped open as she looked at Diamond. Whatever life she had left had officially been sucked out of her. Quinn grabbed her stomach and heaved.

"I'm gonna be sick, I can't listen to any more of this, I have to go," Quinn spoke in disgust, leaning her body up from the desk as she rushed for the back door. Andre moved into her, blocking her path.

"Don't leave me again," he begged. "Please? I know this looks bad, but-" the tears that immediately flooded from Quinn's face stopped his speech.

"I have to get out of here, *now.*" Quinn's hands shook as she held one over her chest, and the other in front of her to block her cheating husband from coming any closer.

"No," he spoke firmly, turning to face the other two women. His eyes turned bloodshot red and his pulse raced. "You both need to get out. Right now," he pointed toward the side door, attempting to keep his composure. Andrea slowly began walking towards it. Diamond looked at Quinn in fear, as Andre moved over to quickly shield his battered wife. Diamond was a whore, but not a fighter. Quinn looked as if she could lose whatever piece of her mind she had left at any minute, and Diamond wanted to make sure she was ready, just in case. Diamond slowly backed herself into the door as Andrea turned around to face her ex-lover.

"I'm going to get you your stupid blood-" hearing Andrea's voice again caused Andre to snap. His eyes widened like a deranged psychopath.

"Get out!!" He hollered at the top of his lungs, looking at the women like he was the devil reincarnated. Both women jumped in fear and ran for the door at the same time. Swinging it open, they darted out. Quinn hastily walked around the side of Andre, trying to make her way to the door as well, but he flooded her path and grabbed her.

"Quinn please, let me explain," he pleaded, as tears instantly rushed to his face.

"Who *are* you??" Her voice shook. A tear fell from Andre's face, watching his wife stare at him in confusion as if she had no idea who he was.

"Baby, just trust me," he stared intensely into her eyes and gripped her shoulders to prevent her from walking away. "Do you trust me?" Quinn stared at her husband...

20 years ago"

Quinn stood lifelessly in her parent's basement with her white Graduation Cap and Gown on. She stood in the exact spot where her mother's dead body had been removed by paramedics a few hours prior. Tears streamed down her face like a river as she weaved in place holding her father's loaded revolver to her head. She had just graduated high school, the valedictorian of her class. She had a full scholarship to Virginia State University for her excellent grades, but neither of her parents were there to see it. Quinn loved her father. He was her first hero and her first love. She always did the best she could in school because she loved to see him smiling from ear to ear when her teachers raved about her at report card conferences. After finding out sixteen years later that her father wasn't really her father, he cut off all communication with her and changed his number. Quinn also loved her mother. Before Eden and Pandora, her mother was her best friend. Her mother was one of the top medical doctors in the nation, and Quinn wanted to be just like her. Quinn's mother could do it all. She went to work with her a lot, watching her mother deliver babies, raise the dead, and heal the sick. Her mother went to Virginia State University on the same Scholarship Quinn had earned, but she never found out because she killed herself before the ceremony had even begun.

"Quinn!?" A male voice called from the top of the basement steps. She could hear them shuffling under the police tape as they rushed to the bottom of the stairs. Quinn turned her head to see Andre. He shuffled back a step and widened his eyes in fear. His body frozen in place. "Baby, what are you doing? Where did you get a gun?"

"Leave me alone." Quinn cried, "stay away from me. Just go." After regaining feeling in his legs, Andre slowly stepped down the last step and walked toward Quinn. He froze in his tracks when he heard the gun cock. "Andre, I mean it," her chin trembled, as she cried. "Get away from me!"

Andre felt a painful tightness in his throat.

"Mannequin, put the gun down, please. Don't do this. You have your whole life ahead of you."

"What life? My entire life has been a lie. Spots flashed in Quinn's vision as she dredged up history with spinning thoughts. Seeing the gut-wrenching pain in his girlfriend's eyes and the gun pointed to her head broke Andre's heart. "I don't understand why everybody keeps lying to me?" She sobbed, "am I not worth the truth?"

"Baby," Andre spoke softly.

"I have nothing left, but me."

"And me," Andre proclaimed. "I need you, you can't leave me here alone. I want to marry you one day and start a family. I know it hurts, but we can get through it together. If you shoot yourself, I'm going to shoot myself, too. I don't want to live without you." Hurt filled his eyes, as his hands clenched into fists. Quinn shook her head as she backed further away from Andre. She wanted to pull the trigger, but her fingers grew numb and she dropped the gun. She felt the room begin to spin, and she plummeted to the floor. Andre darted over and caught her before she fell. The agonizing cry she belted out hurt Andre to his core. He squeezed her tightly, biting his lip to keep himself composed.

"It's okay," he assured her. "You have me. I'll never hurt you. I'll never lie to you. Just trust me baby. Do you trust me?"

A deep, baritone voice bought her back to reality. Quinn blinked her eyes as Andre stood in front of her with pleading eyes.

"Do you trust me?"

Quinn felt sick to her stomach. This was Deja Vu for her all over again. Broken promises, hidden secrets, lies and having someone make a fool out of all the love she invested.

"I have to go before I lose my mind," she stuttered, "I can't be here right now." She immediately rushed to the side of Andre and bolted through the side exit of his office. The second she closed his door and made it to the back of the parking lot, she bent over and vomited.

Chapter 19

Ruby anxiously stood in the checkout line of the same Babies R Us her daughter had gone into labor at just 2 hours prior. The line in the front of the store was held up to the back of the building with irritated customers, waiting their turn for service. Restlessly tapping her foot on the floor, Ruby hunched over against the shopping cart she pushed that held a large car seat box inside of it.

"This is beyond ridiculous," she fussed, glancing over to the left to see what the holdup was.

"Tell me about it," a woman standing behind Ruby shook her head angrily. "I keep hearing they don't have enough workers in the store."

"It's eleven o'clock in the morning, they just opened two hours ago," Ruby hissed, "how can they be short staffed at eleven o'clock?"

The woman laughed.

"I used to work retail back in the day, so I definitely understand the struggle."

"Well praise God for your understanding, but they need to come on." The woman raised her eyebrows, giving Ruby a faint smile.

"I was just trying to help. I apologize." Ruby turned to face the woman, immediately feeling bad for her rudeness.

"I'm sorry. It's not you, today just doesn't seem to be my day. I lost my phone. I'm supposed to be meeting my daughter for lunch, and I can't call her. Then,

I missed the sale for this car seat she wanted," Ruby pointed to her shopping cart, "so now I have to pay full price for it, and of course the checkout line wants to be from here to Kingdom Come."

The woman chuckled again.

"I'm not having the best morning either." She stuck out her hand. "I'm Ashley." Ruby gave Ashley a quick once over before extending her hand. Ashley was a thin, mocha-toned woman that looked to be in her mid to late thirties. Her hair was pulled back into a sloppy ponytail and her facial features were very strong. If it weren't for the orange sundress she wore, Ruby could have easily mistaken her for a man.

"Ruby. Nice to meet you," Ruby smiled. Ashley looked at the car seat in the shopping cart and smiled.

"How old is the baby?"

"She's still in the oven. My daughter is eight months pregnant," Ruby gleamed cheerfully.

"Oh, how wonderful," Ashley squealed. "Do you have any other grandchildren?"

"No, I only have one daughter, and this will be my first grandchild," Ruby smiled.

"That's exciting. I have two sons. One is ten, and the other is six. My mother still spoils them like crazy."

"I'm anticipating those days," Ruby reminisced with a smile plastered across her face. Suddenly, a stocky African American male dressed in all black, with a hoodie covering his head, backed into them.

"Excuse you," Ruby stepped back with her hand out in front of her to stop the man from stepping on her feet. The man turned around, quickly causing Ruby and Ashley to gasp. There were tattoos of teardrops under his eyes, as he nervously met Ruby and Ashley's frightened stare.

"Excuse me," the man said in a low tone. He quickly lowered his head and moved around the two women. He turned back to give them one last stare before disappearing down an aisle. His disheveled appearance made Ruby and her new friend very uncomfortable.

"Jesus Christ," Ruby touched her chest, trying to calm her racing heart.

"These men in those hoodies, walking up on people like that," Ashley shook her head, eyeing the aisle the man walked through, "scares me to death."

"Tell me about it," Ruby replied, trying to shake the fear off her.

"Ladies and Gentlemen, may I please have your attention?" The manager yelled from the front of the store as everyone began to quiet down to hear him talk. "A prisoner has escaped from the Bedford County Prison and is on the loose." Loud gasps and questions began swarming from the crowded store. "The city is getting ready to go into lockdown. We're asking that everyone exit the store and go to your homes, or someplace safe until they have been recaptured."

"Oh no." Ruby's eyes grew wide and her legs almost buckled beneath her as she quickly remembered the suspicious man that nervously pushed pass her a few seconds ago.

"*That man,*" Ashley confirmed in fear.

"Honey, that's my cue to get the hell out of here. It was nice talking to you, Ashley." Ruby walked around her cart and began rushing past the customers who were also in a hurry to exit the building.

"Wait!" Ashley nervously called to Ruby, "I caught the bus here. Do you think you could give me a ride someplace? Like a bus stop by a police station?"

Ashley asked. Ruby quickly motioned for Ashley to follow her.

"Sure, come on." Ruby swarmed past the remaining people in the store, and high tailed it to her red Chevy Cruze in the parking lot. Ashley trailed behind her, panting out of breath.

"I mistook you for a woman in her fifties, But I doubt you're fifty, running that fast," Ashley laughed.

"I am an out of shape, forty-five-year-old woman with high blood pressure and bad knees, but I will turn into an Olympic sprinter to get away from trouble," Ruby laughed.

"Should we have said something to someone about that weird looking guy in the store?" Ashley asked nervously as Ruby flung her keys out of her purse, and unlocked her car door.

"No. If that was who they were looking for, then we need to be far away from here instead of trying to be a hero. The police can handle it." Ashley opened up the passenger door and got in just as Ruby dove in on her driver's side. "How the heck does a prisoner escape from prison, anyway?" Ruby asked, closing her car door before sticking her key into the ignition. She reached to the left for her seatbelt and turned to the right to adjust it, just in time to see Ashley pointing a gun at her torso.

"*The same way they just got into your car.*" The friendly appearance on Ashley's face disappeared into a grimacing stare, "they appear harmless, and make friends." Before Ruby could react, Ashley fired two shots from her nine millimeter handgun right into Ruby's side. The impact caused Ruby's body to slam against the inside of the doorframe.

"Sorry lady," Ashley responded coldly. She reached over and grabbed Ruby's door handle, opening the door. She quickly pushed her lifeless body out of the car.

"Congrats to your daughter...*and* condolences." Ashley slammed the car door and got into the driver's seat. She quickly put Ruby's car in drive and sped off, causing the car tires to screech. Pedestrians swarming into the parking lot after their cars immediately noticed Ruby's body lying on the ground, as blood began to trickle out of her side. "Oh my Goodness!" An elderly woman hollered. "Someone is hurt!"

"She fell out of that red car up there!" A man pointed at the getaway car racing through the parking lot. An unmarked police car doing well above the speed limit in a parking lot wildly drove up to the scene where people began to scream. The man in the hoodie and black jeans jumped out. His partner quickly followed.

"FBI!" one of the men hollered, holding up his badge for the forming crowd.

"She fell out of a moving car. A red Chevy, I think. It went that way!" Someone yelled. The undercover officer looked down at Ruby's body.

"I *knew* that was her!" He said to his partner "I bumped into her on purpose in the store, to see if she'd give me some kind of suspicious look. But I wasn't too sure and didn't want to cause a scene if I was wrong." His face turned red as he kneeled down to Ruby and placed two fingers on her neck. "Dammit!" He hollered, as his partner ran to his car to phone an ambulance.

"We need an ambulance on broad and south, and armed backup going West, toward Baker. The prisoner is armed and dangerous, driving a stolen red Chevy!"

At the hospital.

Eden gaped her body up on the bed in the large birthing room of the hospital. There were two white chairs by the window. One was reserved for Jackson, and the other, for Ruby. Both of them were empty. Aside from the beeping sounds of the monitor above her hospital bed, the room was depressingly quiet. The painful contractions that swept through her pelvis like lightning every twelve minutes, were unbearable. She reached over on her right side to grab her mother's hand for support, but no one was there except the bed rail. Her best friends were missing, her mother wouldn't answer the phone, and Jackson was a gazillion miles away. Everyone that promised to be there for her, were nowhere to be found. Gripping the sides of the bed rails, Eden braced herself and hollered, as another wave of contractions surfaced. The minute they subsided, tears streamed down her face. She was heartbroken and in the worst pain of her life. Just then, the door of her hospital room opened, and she gasped, turning her head to face it.

"Mom!" She hollered, her eyes widening. Her heart nearly fell into her lap when she realized it was just the nurse.

"Hi. It's me again. How are you doing?" The nurse responded cheerfully.

"I just want my mom," Eden began to cry, "Or my friends. *Somebody.*"

The nurse could feel Eden's crushed heart, and she felt bad for her.

"Sweetie, we've called all the numbers you've given us and left messages. We haven't heard anything back."

"This isn't like my mom to just go missing. We were supposed to meet for lunch. She always has her phone. Can someone keep trying?" Eden pleaded, "I can't deliver this baby alone."

"Sure. I'll have somebody try again right now," the nurse said softly.

"Wait," Eden gasped. "My best friend's husband is the Pastor of Tabernacle Church of God in Christ. Is there any way someone can call their church? Maybe she just doesn't have her phone." The nurse's face lit up.

"Dr. Mannequin Bentley?" The nurse asked

"Yes, That's her."

"Oh, I love her! She comes here all the time to pray for the people in the cancer center. Sweetest woman in the world."

"And my other friend, her name is Joanna. She's a lawyer. I don't know her office number, but I'm sure someone can find it to see if she's there." The nurse's mouth gaped open.

"That fire breathing dragon in a human body is your *friend?*" The nurse asked in shock. "Joanna Wilson.

"Yes," Eden's face twisted into a pained look as more contractions flooded her uterus. "That's her. Can somebody please call them? *Please.*" The nurse went to exit the room but she paused, flinching her head back slightly.

"Wait. Didn't she just get married?" The nurse asked, "Joanna?"

"Huh?" Eden looked up. "No. We're not talking about the same person then."

"You're talking about that lawyer from the Pickett case? Light brown skin, about five-foot-four, maybe? Thin and foxy, with all the attitude, right?" The nurse narrowed her eyes.

"Yeah," Eden squinted, "that's her, but she didn't get *married*."

"No, she did. It was on CNN about an hour ago. She was in the airport with some big, tall handsome guy with long hair, coming in from Puerto Rico. The Paparazzi were congratulating her on her wedding." Eden froze. Her chest began to tighten. "That *is* who you're referring to, correct?" Eden gave the nurse a blank look. She opened her mouth, but nothing came out. There was no way Pandora would marry her daughter's father. Eden shook her head quickly in a panic, as her body temperature began to elevate.

"That's- That not her." The audible stress in her voice caused the nurse to frown.

"Are you okay, sweetheart?" The nurse asked with a look of concern. Eden gave the nurse a distant gaze, as her breathing sped up and everything went black.

8 months ago...

Eden and Christopher stretched out on a white hammock that hung from the two trees in the park of Ruby's complex. Christopher ran his fingers through her medium, waist-length braids as Eden rested her head in his lap. A pregnancy test that read "pregnant", dangled in her hand, periodically scraping the ground as her arm swayed in motion with the hammock.

"This is really happening baby," Eden gleamed with a twinkle in her eyes. Her cheeks hurt from smiling so much, as she gazed into the night sky, thinking about her future

with the man of her dreams. "Can you believe it?" She squealed, turning her head to meet his gaze. Biting his lip into a wavering smile, Christopher sat in silence. He was anything but happy.

"Yeah. It's. This is amazing," he stuttered softly with a tone that lacked enthusiasm.

"I always dreamed about the day we would have children" Eden smiled with a radiant glow, "I know we've had our ups and downs, and you and my mom don't really get along, but God does everything for a reason," she nodded. "I think this is the change we need to fix our relationship."

Christopher sighed quietly as his eyes nervously trailed around the area. He was head over heels in love with another woman and had finally proposed to her. He had come over to Eden's house to break off their relationship, and move on with his life, but after being met at the door with a smile, and three positive pregnancy tests, how could he dump her now? Christopher wasn't ready to father a child whose mother he didn't love, but he had no choice.

"Maybe," he replied hesitantly, using one of his hands to rub the back of his neck. Noticing his short words, and distance, Eden lifted her head up to face him.

"What's the matter? You don't sound happy at all?" Christopher pursed his lips and shrugged.

"I just don't think I'm ready to be a father." He lowered his head to face her, "just like I don't think we're really compatible for one another."

Eden rolled her eyes.

"Here we go again." Lifting herself off of him, she sat up on the hammock. "You do this after every argument, Christopher. One minute you love me, the next you're ready to dump me. What is it that you're so afraid of?" She asked impatiently.

"I'm not afraid of anything." He replied, offended by her irritation. "Eden, we argue every other day. We have sex, we make up, and then two days later we're back at it again. I can't take this immaturity. It's getting old, and I'm not getting any younger." Eden jerked her head back and widened her eyes.

"So now I'm immature?"

"I didn't say that," he replied, annoyed

"Last week it was my controlling mother that turned you off. The week before last, it was our communication that was off. This week my age is the issue." She roughly got up from the hammock.

"Eden,"

"No. This," she pointed her fingers back and forth between the two of them, "this is what's getting old, Chris. There is a baby involved now, and someone with your background should know how it feels to grow up with parents who don't have your best interest at heart." She glared at him with cold, flinty eyes. "I didn't ask to get pregnant, but it happened, so that makes me a mother now. I don't want my child to grow up in a broken home with parents who are fighting every other day. My parents went through that, and it was horrible. If you don't know what you want from me, from us, then I'm just going to get an abortion and you can go on about your merry old life." Christopher's head jerked up at her the second he heard "abortion". Even though he had eyes for another woman, the baby growing in Eden's belly had nothing to do with that. Christopher had done a lot of dirt in his lifetime but killing his son or daughter because they wouldn't fit in with his life plans was something he would never forgive himself for. He didn't want that on his heart. He made a baby, so now it was time to be a father. He jumped off the hammock and grabbed Eden's hand.

"Abortion is not an option," he said quickly. "Look, I'm sorry. I'm just..." He stared into her eyes "I'm afraid of commitment," he lied, but I'll figure it out. I am happy about the baby. Whether I'm ready or not, let's do it." He half smiled, instantly regretting his lies. Eden's face lit up as a smile spread across her face.

"Are you sure? Because I love you, and there's nothing I want more than to start a family with you."

"I'm positive baby," he assured her, leaning in to plant a kiss on her forehead. Letting go of her hand, he stepped back and sat back on the hammock. Eden stared down at the pregnancy test one last time before slipping it into her back pocket.

"I'm so excited. What if it's a boy? Should we name him Christopher Jr.?" She climbed onto Christopher, straddling him while her hands slid around his neck. Christopher grinned, showing all thirty-two of his teeth at the thought of having a son named after him.

"That would be so cool. Christopher Jr." he chuckled. "The world could use another me."

"I wonder what labor is going to be like," Eden grimaced, "my mom told me it's the worst pain a woman could feel. She also said that my dad was late getting to the hospital, so she delivered me alone."

Christopher wrapped his hands around Eden's waist, pulling her closer to him.

"Well you don't have to worry about that. I'd never miss my baby's birth. I'll be right there with you. Just like I'm right here now."...

A surge of pain ripped through Eden's uterus. She opened her eyes to see her hospital bed being rushed down a long hallway. Three doctors, and two nurses followed the bed with a look of concern on their faces.

"What's happening?" Eden spoke in a faint voice, barely audible from the oxygen mask that covered her mouth.

"You fainted, and the baby's heart rate dropped. We're going to have to do an emergency C section right now."

"Somebody grab that elevator!" A doctor yelled.

Chapter 20

Pandora used her carryon luggage to shield her face from the dozen news reporters and cameramen swarming her and Jackson as they rushed through the Norfolk, Virginia Airport, en route to the exit. The second her plane took off from Puerto Rico, Pandora realized she'd left her purse in the restaurant. After hearing about the amazing food in the airport restaurant, Tracey decided to swing back for a bite to eat. One of the staff members remembered seeing her and Pandora conversing, and gave her Pandora's possessions the minute she recognized her familiar face. *Tracey had hit the jackpot of revenge*. She searched through Pandora's belongings, fishing for something incriminating. The cold smile that plastered across her face, burst into shocked, ugly laugher as she came across Pandora's marriage certificate. Pandora's body nearly collapsed in on itself the second she exited her aircraft and was ambushed by photographers. She bum-rushed the media, barricading her way through them.

"Put some pep in your step, please. The quicker we get out of here, the quicker they'll leave us alone," Pandora bellowed through clenched teeth, tugging Jackson's arm. Annoyed, Jackson furrowed, allowing himself to be pulled through the airport like a rag doll.

"Yes, mother," he muttered, loud enough for her to hear. Biting her lip, Pandora shut her eyes tight, forcing herself not to cause a scene and give the press an even juicer show. She was fed up with Jackson's smart remarks and his attitude. This was not what she signed up for, and the look on her face showed it. The second they were out of the door, Pandora put her finger up to signal a taxi cab driver, just as the news cameras rushed up to her.

"Joanna, congratulations on your wedding, can you give us a statement?" One reporter stated, shoving his microphone into her face.

"The statements we got from your wedding planner said that it was just the two of you and that it was planned last week. Is that true?" A woman asked as a cameraman flashed his lens in her face. Pandora's soul nearly jumped out of her body.

"I don't have any statements to give right now. Move along, please," she offered a fake smile, using every ounce of patience she had left to keep her composure.

"You're quite the popular woman, Joanna. I'm sure you have lots of friends, were you *trying* to keep your wedding a secret?" Another reporter asked, ignoring her remark. Pandora's expression grew tight. Her muscles did cartwheels in her body. Every vein in her neck began to pulse as she drew in a slow, steady, breath, turning to face the crowd.

"You know what, I have the right to be left alone, and I am exercising that right," she pointed furiously, as the cameras continued to snap pictures of her disheveled demeanor. "That means you are now unlawfully intruding into my private affairs, and with a lot of *balls* to do this to a lawyer," she hissed. "I will sue every last one of you people for slander, invasion of privacy, and defamation of character," her temper began to surface, "I will sue the sorry people you work for. Shoot, I'll even find a way to sue the workers responsible for cementing the concrete you're *standing* on," she roared, gritting her teeth as the cameramen backed up, and the reporters lowered their microphones. Jackson looked on in concern, hoping she didn't do anything she would regret.

"Are you aware that Ashley Peterson has escaped from the county correctional facility?" A bold reporter broke through the silence. The hurricane building inside of her quickly faded. Pandora's blinked at the reporter's remark, blankly staring in confusion.

"What?" She hesitated. Suddenly, a black limo pulled up to the curb. Two, six-footfive bodyguards in black suits got out and made their way to her.

"Ms. Wilson? Or is it Mrs. Ford, now?" A guard asked. Pandora narrowed her eyes as Jackson looked between the two in confusion.

"Yes?" she replied impatiently.

"We have been sent to keep you in protective custody until Ashley Peterson has been detained." Jackson looked on in confusion.

"She escaped? When?" Pandora frowned. The other guard grabbed her and Jackson's bags, placing them in the trunk.

"Early this morning. She's already killed a woman and stolen her car. We're uncertain as to her whereabouts, or if you're even someone she's looking for, but considering you're the one who put her away, we want to protect you." Pandora stood dumbfounded as the nosy reporters shoved their microphones in her face, asking a million new questions.

"Wait, so where are we going? I need to get to the hospital. My dau—" Pandora snapped her head toward Jackson, her eyes nearly bulging out of their sockets, as he quickly caught himself. "I—I mean, I need to get to an ill family member."

"We are set to take her home and stand guard until the prisoner has been detained," the guard responded boldly, opening the door for them to get in. Pandora was still speechless, but immediately obeyed the guard's orders. Jackson sighed, deciding to obey. The minute the door was shut, he angrily punched the bulletproof window.

"You've got to be kidding me!" He fussed.

"Can this day get any freaking worse?" Pandora shook her head, shoving herself into the seat.

"My phone is dead. Yours is too. I can't even call Eden and tell her any of this!" Jackson said.

"Ooh, no worries, I'm pretty sure she'll find out the second she turns on the television," Pandora replied calmly. "Goodbye reputation...*Goodbye Eden*." The limo began to move as she sat in a daze. Her worst nightmares were coming true right in the public eye.

"Oh, right," Jackson spat angrily, "Eden will find out you got married, and it'll wreck your little fake friendship. Meanwhile, I'm missing the birth of my daughter. A memory I can never get back."

"Jesus Christ," she huffed, wailing her hands into the air, "why couldn't we be in separate cars?"

"Ditto!" He shouted.

"Separate cars, separate homes, separate lives!" Pandora exploded.

"Of course, because running is your answer to *every* problem you can't control!" he rebutted.

"You don't know me," she gritted

"That's your problem. *Nobody knows you.* Maybe if you let go of your insecurities and let people in, they could *get* to know you!" Pandora's eyes slowly widened. If looks could kill, Jackson would have dropped dead.

"I regret marrying you, I don't know what I ever saw in you," she responded coldly, "I hate you. I should have never-"

"You hate me, but you stayed with me when I lied to your face?" Jackson hissed, deliberately raising his eyebrows at her. "I played you for years, Ms. Attorney, and you *let* me. I was the dog you knew I was, and you cried over me and still stayed. You ran off and married me, and you ruined a close friendship over me," he laughed with an edge. "Let's be real baby, you don't *hate* me, you love me; because you can't -*control* me." Pandora grimaced, shooting Jackson a dismissive chuckle.

"Please, that is not the-" an irate Jackson angled his body, giving Pandora direct probing eye contact.

"You cannot manipulate me, your inflated ego does not bother me, and your temper doesn't scare me. You can't read me like a book, you have no idea what I'm going to do or say next, and that secretly excites you," he scolded. Jackson was one hundred percent right, but Pandora was too prideful to admit it. Pandora was the queen of manipulation and facades. At fifteen years old, a couple that lived next door, whom she loved so much, kidnapped her. When her parents weren't home, they would always invite her over and kept her entertained. They helped her with her homework, gave her money to go to the store, and saw to it that she was fed, bathed, and sent to bed if her mother was too late getting home. One day as she stood on her porch steps, she was snatched from behind and dragged into a cellar where she was locked away and hidden from the rest of the world. For almost nine months, Pandora was beaten, starved, psychologically damaged, and molested. For months, she heard her mother above the dungeon next-door, crying, kicking, and screaming as she cooperated with the police and the community to find their missing little girl. Pandora tried signaling for their attention, but nobody could see her. After three months of no luck, her parents, along with the rest of the world assumed she had died, and mourned her death. After their grieving process was over, her face went on a milk carton with all the other missing kids, and everyone eventually went back to their daily lives. Pandora lived in a corner of the large, dark basement with sewer rats, and all sorts of other disgusting animals, wishing someone would come save her. She could hear her brother, as he sat outside with his friends eating ice cream and laughing. She could hear her parents engaging in their day-to-day activities, loving on one another. Everyone seemed to forget about her, except her friends. The community built a shrine of balloons and teddy bears by the curb of her home. Every single day for nine months, Quinn came and sat by the curb after school, and talked to Pandora as if she were right there. She cried, she laughed and pleaded with God to find her best friend. Eden came by with her mother at least twice a week to put new teddy bears down, and keep her memory alive. Pandora swore that dungeon would be her grave, until nine months later. Her neighbor's husband had come home drunk. He staggered down into the dungeon, as he had done every night to relieve his erection, but this time he passed out after the fact. Pandora was able to run up the stairs, and out of the house, screaming for dear life. Both of her neighbors were eventually tried in court, but they had a good lawyer who somehow proved that they suffered from mental issues. They were sent to an insane asylum for a year, and let back into society. Physically, Pandora was free, but mentally, she suffered for years after that. Anger, revenge, and control fueled her. She went to law school and became a force to be reckoned with. Since there was no justice for her, she made sure there would be no justice for anyone else. She was every criminal's hero, and every innocent victim and their family's worst nightmare. Pandora was an impossible act to follow. There was nobody in the world that could stand toe to toe with her, *except Jackson*. His resistance to give in to her defense mechanisms pissed her off, but it also turned her on. Pandora's anger began to subside as she peered up at his handsome face, and she fell in love all over again. His superiority radiated through his posture, giving her no choice but to give in. He stared at her with a boldness that meant business. Her facial features softened and her eyes stared at him with an instant vulnerability. It was crazy how much power he had over her. Jackson had turned her world upside down within a matter of weeks, but her heart was beating and begging for him as if everything were okay.

"I'm sorry," she spoke softly, swallowing her pride. "I'm sorry. It's been a long day." Jackson felt like crap. He was only trying to prove a point; he didn't mean to hurt her feelings. He slid closer to her, wrapping his arm around her neck.

"Who is Ashley, anyway?" Jackson asked in a calm voice, hoping to change the subject.

"A client I represented a couple years ago," she replied faintly, staring straight ahead. "She butchered her whole family after finding out her husband had an affair. The kids, the mother in law, *and* the dog. I almost got her off on temporary insanity, but-" Pandora paused as water filled her eyes and a tear trickled down before she could catch it.

"But what?" Jackson asked.

"As I stood in the courtroom that day, cross-examining her psychologist, I turned to face the jury," she reminisced, biting her lip as she formed a smug grin. "I knew just what I needed to say to manipulate the situation and win them over. And when I looked up to face them, I saw the most beautiful man I had ever laid eyes on," she chuckled as more tears trailed from her eyes. "Those gorgeous eyes and strong cheekbones wiped my entire memory," she nodded, wiping her tears. "I forgot *everything* and lost. My first case ever," she shook her head as she turned to face Jackson who stared in disbelief.

"I saw you on TV one day and just wanted to be in your presence. I bargained like crazy with this guy to get a seat on the jury. I don't remember anything about the case, I was lost in you the whole time. Once we locked eyes, that was it for me," Jackson smiled, "everything went black, and I had to get up out of there. I never knew you lost the case. I dipped out before deliberation."

"Well, from my perspective, I guess I didn't really see it as a loss, because I," she hesitated. "I found you," she blushed. "There was a hint of mystery in your eyes back then that I couldn't exactly put my finger on at the time, but now I know it was nothing but the devil," she laughed at herself as Jackson chuckled with a smirk. "There's just something about you I can't get enough of," she sighed, staring into his khaki-colored eyes. "You drive me *crazy*."

Jackson moistened his lips and leaned in to her personal space.

"And you can't stop yourself from not being able to do anything about it." Pandora took in a soft breath as Jackson's hot spearmint breath traveled through her ear and set fire to her insides. His deep, baritone voice alone could drive her crazy, if he talked long enough. Biting his lip, he leaned over to make sure the partition separating them from the guards in the front seat was secure. Sliding the spaghetti straps to her dress down to her forearms, Jackson kissed her bottom lip, her cheek, and then her shoulders, leaving behind a trail of fire everywhere he touched.

"Wait," Pandora protested, nervously staring out of the windows while the limo drove through the crowded city. "This is a federal limousine. We could go to jail. There could be cameras in here... *anything*." Jackson's eyes bore into hers, allowing her a moment of silence to think about just who she was talking to. Jackson was the king of spontaneity. In his world, there was no such thing as rules, modesty, or dignity; *there was only love.* Love does what it wants, where it wants, as loud as it wanted. He reached down and kissed her. Their lips passionately clung to each other like a lifeline, as she let out a breathless moan. Pandora was quite the instrument to play, so finely tuned, and if you pressed the right buttons, she made the most *beautiful* sounds.

The noisy, public atmosphere around them grew louder as the limo stopped at a red light. Shielded by only a tinted window, and a soundproof partition, Pandora released her inhibitions, and made the sweetest love to her husband, right there in the limo.

Although nothing was going right, their bodies *never* got it wrong. When they had their hands on each other, they both knew they were where they needed to be.

Chapter 21

After parking her car in Pandora's garage, Quinn got out and slowly walked around to the front of Pandora's home where she had been staying. She knew her body was moving, but physically, she couldn't feel her limbs. She was staring straight ahead of her, but couldn't see anything. It appeared as if her very soul had been sucked out of her body. Her dead, vacant eyes held no life. Her chest heaved up and down, slowly gasping for air. *"This can't be real,"* she thought to herself over and over again, recalling the events that had taken place in her husband's office. She didn't understand. It was like her brain short-circuited and needed to be rebooted. She reached the top of Pandora's steps and used her keys to unlock the door. Stumbling like a functioning alcoholic, Quinn left the door open and the keys dangling from the keyhole as she walked over to Pandora's couch in one of the living rooms. Around her, everything seemed to be moving in fast-forward, while she stood motionless in the middle of it all. Quinn tried to sit down, but it was more like a stumble and fall onto the off white, Victorian-style couch.

"What has happened to my life?" She spoke softly, pressing the heels of her hands into her eyes until she saw nothing but sparkles. An image of her sorry husband and the way he stared at her with a guilty expression flashed in her mind. Immediately, she started to cry. Quinn never asked to be the First

Lady of a church. She promised to love, honor, and obey her husband, *not a pastor*. She went to church on Sundays and holidays, but that was it. When she married Andre, she had plans to travel the world, raise their children, and build an empire with the man she loved. Instead, she ended up on a pulpit, praying for the sick, feeding the hungry, fixing marriages, casting out demons, and leading people to Christ. There were clothes she couldn't wear, places she could no longer go, and words she couldn't say anymore because of who she had become. Her best friends meant the world to her, but time with them became extremely limited due to her ministry. Still, Quinn never complained. She gave selflessly of herself because she loved her husband, and the low down, disrespectful way he repaid her, was a slap in the face. Cupping her face into her hands, Quinn rocked back and forth, shaking her head, begging God to make her stop loving him. Joseph stood silently in Pandora's foyer. He had been in a different room the entire time thinking about his own marriage before he heard Quinn's painful tears. Out of all the years he had known her, he had never seen her without a smile on her face. Quinn was an image of perfection, poise, and grace. Seeing her broken down and weak caused his heart to ache.

"Hey," he spoke softly, as his voice cracked. Quinn heard someone say something, but she was too distraught to look up. She didn't know who it was, and at this point, she didn't care. Joseph walked over to Quinn and slowly sat down beside her. "If it makes you feel any better, I feel the exact same way." Using his hands, he softly caressed her back, as Quinn did the best she could to wipe her face before sitting up to face Joseph.

She lifted her face to meet him, and it was like Joseph could almost see the scars of horror etched into her eyes. They were cold and gray, like the cement on the floors of a jail cell. He gazed at her and saw a sad, pleading soul. He saw grief. He saw darkness. *It was earth-shattering.*

"I talked to my wife a little while ago," he muttered, "she told me everything that happened. I came here to talk to my sister," he paused, shaking his head. "I want a divorce...but, how are you?" He asked. He watched Quinn's eyes widen, openly staring at him like she could slap him for asking her such a stupid question. "Never mind, it's evident that you-" he rubbed the back of his neck, not knowing what else to say.

"There is a guy at my church who served in the army for almost fifteen years," Quinn spoke, training her eyes on a glass vase on the table in front of her. "As a favor to him, I counsel most of the soldiers in his sector that have fought in Iraq. Many of them have been exposed to bombs, dead children, bodies all over the place, but they didn't have the time to psychologically process it, because they were still fighting, and killing. Once they came home and tried to go back to their normal lives, they began to re-experience it, and some of them nearly lost their minds. They suffered from what's called, Post Traumatic Stress Disorder," tears began trickling down her face as Joseph used his fingers to wipe them away. "I spent the last twenty-five years of my life, head over heels in love, and I found out a week ago that it was all in vain. Six months ago, my husband just changed up on me. I tried to make sense of it, but I didn't understand it, so I continued on in my daily life being superwoman. Now, as the plot thickens, I'm beginning to re-experience all of it," she gestured with her finger. "The things I feel in the moments of finding out my love and my marriage was a fluke, I swear, is equivalent to anything that happens to a soldier on the battlefield."

"I understand," Joseph nodded. "Andrea didn't cheat on me, but she lied to me for years. Trust is everything in a relationship. If she can look me in my face and lie about a child, what else is she capable of hiding? I'm just- I'm ready to be done with marriage. That's it," Joseph said.

"Be careful of the choices you make while you're angry," Quinn responded, almost innately. *Even through her pain, her gift to help others still lived on.*

"She should've been more careful of the choices *she* made when she lied to me for nearly all these years, Joseph spat, "I took her son in, not caring if he was mine or not. I loved him like he was my own, and it wouldn't have mattered if his father were dead or alive. She just keeps lying to me, it's like a snowball effect-"

"Joe," Quinn intervened.

"And the snowball can continue to roll, right on down to divorce court," he huffed.

"Joseph," Quinn replied sternly, as Joseph looked at her. "What therefore God has joined together, let no man separate. That's a biblical order. When you got married, you didn't get married under yourself, you got married under God. Marriage is not of human origin, if it were, then human beings would have the right to throw it away whenever they chose to do so," Quinn's voice shook. She was mentally, and physically falling apart. Speaking life into someone else was the only way she seemed to keep herself together. "Since God is the one who instituted marriage, he is the only one with the authority to determine its standards, set its rules, and do away with it. I'm not telling you what to do, I'm just saying before you make a decision like that, clear your mind, and go to him first." Quinn's voice sounded like a rushing waterfall in Joseph's ears. He loved hearing her talk. He looked over and smiled, reaching out to touch her leg.

"Look, you've done enough. *For everyone.* God is beyond pleased, I'm sure. Stop trying to help me, and let's worry about how we can help *you.* This isn't an issue you can throw into the back of your closet and forget about. Exposure brings closure, didn't you just reference that in your analogy about the soldiers?" Quinn's thoughts immediately began to spin again, but she forced herself to maintain eye contact with Joseph.

"It seems like hiding from your emotions is what you do best. You're a wreck, but I would have never believed it if I didn't see it for myself. This is the first time I'm able to look past your pretty and see your pain," he slid closer. This was the closest they had ever been to one another. *"You're not okay?"*

"I agree, i'm not okay," Quinn replied, "but it's silly for both of us to sit here and just hurt, with no solutions," she blinked, causing more tears to flow from her face. "If I can't fix me, the least I can do is try to help you." Using both of her hands, she wiped her face. Seeing her so flustered and upset made Joseph feel terrible. He wanted to kill Andre.

"What can I do to help?" His eyes bored into hers.

"I don't think there's anything you-" Without thinking, Joseph impulsively leaned in and kissed Quinn's lips. With widened eyes, she sprung up from the couch like a rocket, slightly opening her mouth into a gasp. The minute Joseph realized what he had done, his heart started to race. The look of fear was all over him.

"I'm sorry," he said quickly, getting up from the couch, "Oh, gosh," he rubbed the back of his neck. "I'm so sorry." Quinn stared at him in disbelief. That was the first time another man had touched her lips. Even though it was a stolen kiss, Quinn felt like she had done something wrong. And it felt *good.* Since high school, it wasn't just Joseph that longed for a chance to be with her, it was half the boys in the school. In college, most of Andre's teammates and closest friends threw her subliminal signs that Andre may have been too stupid to realize, but she wasn't. The married men in her congregation and the deacons in ministry all gave her second glances when they noticed Andre wasn't looking. Just as bad as the women wanted Quinn's husband, the men wanted Andre's wife. However, Quinn carried herself like a lady, pretending to be oblivious to the unwanted attention. She knew she was beautiful, and she understood her worth. Her self-esteem and self-respect never needed validation, not even from her husband. But now, she was fed up with playing the fool. Love had made a mockery of her, and her marriage was a lie. It was time for *payback*. Quinn slowly moved into Joseph and fused her lips with his. The kiss she returned nearly took the breath out of his lungs. Her lips were honey sweet, and lilac soft, just like they were in Joseph's dreams. He wrapped his arm around Quinn's waist, as she closed her eyes and welcomed the unfamiliar taste of another man's essence. She slowly opened her mouth, as their tongues intertwined into a seductive dance. Their lips became mesmerized with one another, pressing together time after time until desire ignited in Pandora's living room. Quinn wrapped her arms around Joseph's neck while he backed her into the nearest wall, pressing himself against her. The skin on her arm felt like silk, and he could only imagine how her hands would feel on the rest of him. Joseph broke free from their kiss and began licking, kissing, and nibbling on her neck like he was starving. The feel of his erection against her stomach caused her eyes to open. The realization of what she was getting ready to get into, caused her breathing to become unsteady. Quinn wasn't sure her heart had ever pounded so fast in her life. She wanted so badly to push Joseph off, but the moans of Diamond replayed in her ear like a broken record until Quinn shut her eyes, tilted her head back and forced herself into a sea of lust. He let go of her neck and looked at her with a spicy combination of passion and lust. She could feel the heat from his eyes traveling up and down her body. Their lips re connected, telling a story with their pleasure; *one that could never be told again.* Joseph circled his tongue around Quinn's, and she returned his lewd gesture with her own. *They were playing a wicked game.*

Outside.

The black limousine pulled up in front of Pandora's home. The two guards got out and opened the back door, allowing her and Jackson to get out.

"I don't understand," Jackson huffed. "If the criminal was caught, why couldn't you just take us to the hospital like we asked?"

"We apologize for altering any plans, but it was protocol for us to drop you off at the location we were assigned."

"It's fine. We're here now," Pandora replied, as the guards removed the bags from the trunk and placed them on the sidewalk, "we can put the bags inside and take my car. Thanks again for the protection guys."

"It was our pleasure. You have a good day. Be safe," one of them replied, getting back into the limo, before pulling off.

"I'm so anxious to see my baby," Jackson smiled, "I've been waiting for this moment all day." Pandora was in no hurry to get to the hospital. She had no idea what the news reporters had said about her, or if either of her friends had watched it. Vacation was over, and reality had returned. The guilt of what she had done began to weigh heavily on her mind, as she walked toward her front door. She got to her steps and immediately paused when she realized her door was open.

"What in the world," she stared. Looking to her left, she saw Joseph's car parked a few feet away, just as Jackson had reached the top of her steps.

"Is someone here?" He asked, confused.

"*Looks* like my brother." She rolled her eyes. "He could've at least closed the door behind him." They both walked into her home. Placing her purse on the kitchen island, she walked toward her foyer.

"Joe?" She called, "since when did you start popping up unannounced? Did you lose your phone or break your finger?" She hissed, entering into her living room. Her eyebrows raised and her mouth gaped open when she saw Joseph and Quinn kissing each other. They were so into what they were doing, they had no idea she was even standing there. Jackson crept into the living room behind Pandora, just as Joseph's hands were trailing into Quinn's skirt.

"Wow," Jackson laughed, causing Quinn and Joseph to jump. Quinn's eyes widened in terror the second she saw Pandora. Joseph spun around quickly, scratching his forehead.

"Hey...Anna," he said nervously, looking everywhere but at her.

"Hi," Pandora slyly grinned, squinting her eyes at the two. "Was I interrupting something?" A flush swept across Quinn's face, as her ears reddened and she looked down at the floor.

"No," Joseph quickly cut in, "not at all. I was just..." he glanced nervously at Quinn, putting his hands into his pockets, "I stopped by to talk to you, and you weren't here, so I- I'm just going to use the restroom and head home," he muttered.

"It's nice to meet you, Joseph," Jackson slightly waved with a smirk.

"Hello," Joseph glanced up at him, confused, "and you are...?"

"Jackson." The sound of his name caused Quinn to look up. This was the first time she had ever seen him.

"Nice to meet you, but who are you?" Joseph asked. Jackson cut his eye at Pandora, unsure of how he should introduce himself. Pandora closed her eyes, slumping her hands to her sides. The world already knew her secret; there was no sense in trying to hide it anymore.

"Uh, I'm a client," Jackson replied, unsure of himself.

"He's my husband," Pandora replied faintly, finally dropping her bombshell.

All the blood nearly drained from Quinn's face, as her voice burst into a gasp.

"Since when?" Joseph blurted out, confused, and somewhat angry. His sister was his pride and joy. He couldn't believe she would make a decision like that without consulting him.

"WHAT?" Quinn's high-pitched yell caused everyone to jump.

"We got married the other day in Puerto Rico. Just the two of us," Jackson stated, glancing at Pandora, who looked as if she wanted to disappear and never come back.

"Wow…" Joseph hissed, glaring at his sister. "You sized Andrea up the minute you found out I had a crush on her. I've never even met this guy before," Joseph darted at Jackson.

"Are you *serious*?" Quinn couldn't believe it. Pandora swallowed hard before looking up to face her friend. She walked over to her, grabbing her arm to pull her into another room.

"We should talk. *Now*." Pandora lead Quinn down the hallway into her office.

"Joanna, have you lost your *mind*?!" Quinn roared, entering into Pandora's office. Pandora quickly shut the door. "Please tell me this a joke."

"Quinn, listen, please," Pandora's eyes begged, "I feel terrible enough as it is, don›t make it worse."

"*Worse?* Quinn's eyebrows raised at her nerve, "does Eden know about this? Because if not honey, *worse* hasn't even happened yet." Pandora averted her gaze to the floor, feeling her heart sink to her ankles. She felt like the devil. Quinn covered her mouth in shock, staring at Pandora as if she was a ghost.

"Quinn, you know I would never intentionally do anything to jeopardize my friendship with either of you."

"I understand how you felt about him, but I didn't think you were capable of doing something like this after finding out the truth." Quinn said, "your best friend in the whole world is pregnant with his child, and you went off and married him?" Quinn turned her face up. "That is so *scandalous*, and...*wrong.*"

"Whoa," Pandora huffed, "wait a minute First Lady Holy Ghost, queen of perfection, and all that is righteous," She crossed her arms, "let she who is without sin, cast the first stone. Let's take a look into *your* closet." Quinn's eyes instantly dropped to the floor. "You almost killed your husband in my BMW, and now you're having an affair in my living room with a married man."

"I did not have an *affair*," Quinn looked up, trying to justify her situation as she adjusted her blouse.

"Shoot, you had *something*," Pandora bellowed. "If it wasn't my brother, it would've gotten me all hot and bothered." Quinn folded her arms and looked away from her friend. Embarrassed wasn't the word to describe how she felt. "You feel guilty, don't you?" Pandora's voice cracked, "join the club. I didn't intend to get this deep, as I'm sure you didn't either. There was just something about Jackson that I kept finding myself unable to stay away from. Deep down, I still wrestle with the demons of my past, in feeling forgotten, and abandoned. I walked through much of my adult life with a closed heart, assuming that by doing so, I'd be spared from further pain. But, a closed heart is a broken heart. Ironically, in being tangled up in Jackson's web of lies and deceit, I learned that the only way to handle heartache is to open your heart all the way. It did leave me vulnerable, but it also taught me some lessons. "That man *does* something to me,"

Pandora protested, "he makes me feel alive, he forces me to face my insecurities, and let go of some stuff in order to be a better woman. Love has opened up my world. It saved me. *I needed it."* Quinn listened to Pandora speak from her heart.

"I understand," was the only words she found herself able to speak.

"I chose love over my friend, and it wasn't easy. I'm not sure Eden will ever be able to forgive me for this, but, I made a bold move for myself and I just hope she can understand and want to move forward."

Quinn's heart was crushed for both of her friends. Love had definitely softened Pandora's heart and put her in touch with her harsh reality, Quinn just wished it wasn't the father of Eden's baby. Pandora's door swung open.

"We really should be getting down to the hospital," Jackson stated anxiously, "if I'm lucky, maybe Eden will still be in labor." Quinn's eyes widened.

"Labor? Since when?"

"She left a message on Jackson's phone early this morning saying she was in labor, so we got an early flight back," Pandora stated.

"Oh no," Quinn's heart began to race, as she hurried out of Pandora's office. "I don't have my phone, it's at the church. We need to get to the hospital."

"My sentiments exactly," Jackson hurried behind Quinn. Pandora wiped her face, following everyone into the kitchen.

"Anna, you know your stupid little marriage is all over the news?" Joseph teased, glancing up at the television on her wall.

"*Stupid?"* Jackson intervened, offended.

"Joseph, play nice please," Pandora begged, "I'm in a heap of trouble as it is." Just then, a breaking news bulletin popped on the screen.

"Ashley Peterson, a prisoner that escaped from the Norfolk County Correctional Facility, has been captured and detained by authorities after a nearly two-hour police chase in a red Chevrolet Cruze, that was stolen from a Babies R Us. Police say Peterson got in the car with the owner of the vehicle, before shooting her, and pushing her out of the car. The victim has been identified as fourty-five-year old Ruby Grant, of Richmond, Virginia. She was reported dead at the scene." The terrified gasp Pandora belted out, nearly took all the breath from her body. Quinn screamed to the top of her lungs.

"What!" Joseph yelled.

Everyone bolted for the front door.

Chapter 22

Andre slowly limped through the hallway of the Richmond, Virginia Hospital, attempting to force himself back into reality. Two doctors and a nurse led the way as he trailed behind. He tried his best to focus, but it was almost impossible for him to think straight. His thoughts raced, and his heart pounded. His bad nerves forced his hands to tremble in his pockets. His life had become tangled into a complete mess. There were so many knots, he didn't know which one he should try to unravel first. Still, he was a pastor, and when ministry called, he had no choice but to answer.

"Thank you for coming Pastor Bentley," one of the doctors stopped in front of a hospital room.

"No problem," Andre responded, "what's going on?"

"This woman," the doctor looked down at his clipboard, "Eden Grant. She expressed being a close friend of your wife. Do you know her?"

"I do," Andre affirmed, "she's a very close friend of our family.

"Alright. Well, she came in here this morning, in labor. Her due date wasn't for another month or so, but she was full term, so instead of putting her on steroids and bed rest, we took her to labor and delivery to give birth."

"Okay."

"At some point during the process, the baby's heart rate dropped. We took her up to the OR, for an emergency c-section, but by the time we got the baby out, the little girl's heart had already stopped beating." Andre hunched his posture toward the doctors as his mouth slacked in disbelief. "We tried everything we could to revive the child, but it was too late, and we pronounced her dead."

"Jesus," he hissed.

"It didn't help that she came in here alone asking for her friends, but we were unable to get a hold of anyone. We tried contacting your wife, as she requested, along with some others, but no one responded except you," the doctor stated.

"My wife had an emergency and left the church abruptly this morning. Her things are still in her office, including her phone." Andre replied, "but Eden lives with her mother. Has no one been able to reach her, either? The nurse cupped her mouth and stared down at the floor, shaking her head as the doctor peered up at Andre.

"We couldn't at first, and then paramedics bought her in on a stretcher, with a fatal gunshot wound. Andre stood there trying to remember how to breathe, unable to speak, totally stunned as the news bounced around in his skull. "She was shot by an escaped prisoner," the doctor shook his head. "She shot her, and then stole her car.

"Oh my *Goodness*," Andre stared incredulously, "are you serious...Miss *Ruby*?" He turned away, rubbing a hand down his face as he frantically paced a few steps before walking back to face the doctors.

"With all the physical trauma to Eden's body from the surgery, her vitals are everywhere, and with the mixture of so much tragedy, they are beginning to spike to a dangerous level. Maybe a familiar face or a spiritual prayer can calm her down. If not, we're going to have to sedate her until her levels drop."

"Right," Andre replied in anguish. He stared at Eden's door, forcing himself to remain composed, "I'll see if I'm any help."

"Thanks for your cooperation" they walked away. From the outside, Andre could hear Eden's cries. Shaking his head in despair, he blew out a deep breath, turned the doorknob, and walked in. Eden sat straight up in her hospital bed, rocking back and forth. Periodically, she choked on her cries, mumbling incoherent words. Death wasn't kind. It snatched where it could, taking people who were far too young, far too good. Eden's wide, bloodshot eyes stared at the wall in front of her, but their gaze was unfocused. Her face was sunken and haunted, her mind cold and empty. Ruby promised her daughter that she would always be there for her. Jackson told her that she would never go through childbirth alone. Quinn and Pandora pinky swore with a cherry on top, that even though life took them in different directions, they would always be there for each other in the time of need. Eden's hands trembled, frantically shaking her head in denial. Her rumpled appearance and erratic behavior bought immediate tears to Andre's eyes.

"Eden?" His deep voice filled the room. Eden's eyes slowly regained focused, traveling from the wall, to meet his face. As their eyes locked in on each other, their energy briefly connected. They were both in the midst of a life-altering situation that left them feeling defeated, curled up into a fetal position, wishing they could turn back the hands of time.

"I don't understand," Eden spoke through her tears, "is this really happening to me?" She bore into Andre's eyes, looking for answers. Rushing over to her, Andre wrapped his arms around her. Eden's body nearly collapsed into his embrace. She cried as if her brain were being shredded from the inside. Pain flowed from her every pore. From her mouth, came a cry so raw. Rubbing her back, Andre closed his eyes and thought of his wife. Moments like these reminded him of how much he needed her. Other than reciting a scripture, or speaking a word of encouragement, he had no idea of what else to do. Quinn was his lifeline. She always knew the right words to say and had the perfect warm embrace for every type of situation. Andre just spoke the words, it was his wife's actions that bought them to life. Suddenly, the door to Eden's hospital room swung open, and who else would be standing in the doorway, but the First Lady herself. A tightness grew in her chest the instant she was met with her husband's face, instead of Eden's. She was not mentally prepared to run into him.

"Quinn," Andre turned. Quinn wanted to run as far away from Andre as she could, but she knew this was no time to get caught up in her feelings. Her best friend needed her. She had needed her all morning, and Quinn wasn't there.

"Eden?" She rushed into the room, deliberately ignoring her husband's presence. Quinn looked right through Andre who let go of Eden and stepped back against the wall. He couldn't believe she disregarded his presence.

"Quinn!" Eden hollered. They both grabbed one another, holding on for dear life.

"Honey, I'm *so* sorry I missed everything, I didn't have my phone," tears of guilt immediately rushed down her face.

"How did this happen? I don't understand," Eden fussed, trying to make sense of her reality. "Quinn, this isn't real, wake me up, please," she screamed, clutching her friend as tight as she could. Eden's pain was so deep and agonizing it nearly shook the life out of Quinn. Tears spilled from her face like a dam, as she gasped for air that just wasn't there. "Please, wake me up from this nightmare. I need to talk to my mother and hold my daughter," Eden desperately pleaded.

"I wish I knew the right words to say," Quinn choked down a sob, "but I'm here, I promise." Eden's body trembled in Quinn's arms. Her thoughts raced in circles, and her mind was delirious. She came into the hospital to deliver a baby, but she would be leaving empty-handed. She left the house this morning, telling her mother she would see her at the Red Lobster at noon, not knowing that she would never see her again. Eden was forced into a world forever changed. Suddenly, her life made no sense anymore. Her entire world felt like it was ending, as each breath felt like an effort.

The only announcement of Pandora's arrival into the room was a slight drop in the air temperature, and the descent of absolute silence. She stood there, watching her best friends share a moment she wished so badly she could've been a part of. When Quinn, Joseph, and Jackson reached the floor of Eden's room, the doctors explained everything. Jackson grew delirious. He lost a piece of him that he never even got the chance to meet. The doctors gave him oxygen to help his breathing and wheeled him away into a hospital room. Torn between the two, Pandora had no clue who she should see to first, but Quinn encouraged her to check on her husband. Eden's cries ceased, almost immediately. Slowly letting go of Quinn, her eyes scanned the room until they reached Pandora. The minute Eden saw Pandora's face, anger bubbled up inside of her. Her breathing turned into heavy pants and her hands balled into fists so tight, her knuckles turned ashen white.

"Did you really come here?" Eden scolded. Her immediate shift in emotion caused Andre to look up. Quinn nervously stepped back, cutting her eyes in another direction. Pandora hoped to God that Eden hadn't found out about her and Jackson, especially during a time like this. *But she hoped wrong.* Standing unnaturally still, Pandora pursed her lips, as tears flooded from her face. For the first time in her life, Pandora was speechless. "Why the tears, Anna? I would think you'd be relieved to find out your husband's baby died while I delivered her," she spat with a coldness that froze everyone in the room. Andre jerked his head back and turned to face Pandora. Quinn looked on, horrified, wishing so badly that Pandora would have stayed downstairs with Jackson.

"That's not true," Pandora shook her head. Slowly, she made her way toward Eden's bed. "I'm sorry about all of this, but I *do* care, let me be here for-"

Steam nearly flew out of Eden's ears.

"Stay away from me!!" She roared. Pandora jumped back, and Quinn rushed to the middle of the room between them. Quinn faced Pandora.

"Anna, I think you should just lea-"

"Get the hell out of the way, Quinn!" Eden shouted as Quinn spun around to face her.

"No," She darted, "this is a horrible time to-" Andre quickly walked over to Quinn, aggressively ushering her to the side as he followed. "Andre, stop" Quinn fussed, "this is not okay."

"Let *them* work it out, you can't fix this. Stay out of it," he ordered.

"It'll never be okay!" Eden continued to yell, "there will never be a right time for a friend I have considered a sister since *middle* school, to look me in my face and tell me she married my child's father," her voice lost power with each word she spoke.

Pandora bit her lip and folded her arms, watching Eden with a pained expression, as she vented. Seeing her friend in so much pain ripped her heart to pieces, especially knowing she played a part in it. She loved Jackson so much, but in that moment she regretted the way her heart felt. "I looked up to you! I have fought for you, cried with you, and have been your biggest cheerleader for the last fifteen years! When you were too scared to live in your neighborhood after what happened, my mother opened up her house to you, and you do something like *this*?" Eden winced, disgusted. Pandora walked with an ego the size of a giant, but in that moment she felt like the size of a mustard seed. If there had been a hole nearby, she would have crawled inside of it. Her stomach twisted in knots as her conscious ate her alive from the inside out. Eden's face reddened and her mouth twisted into a snarl, as she glared at Pandora.

"Why couldn't you have done us all a favor and *died* in your neighbor's dungeon?!" Pandora looked like a deer in headlights. Clutching her chest, she stared back at Eden with feverish eyes.

Quinn's jaws nearly dropped to the hospital floor. "That's it, move," she tore away from her husband and rushed over to Pandora.

"Anna, you just need to go." If Pandora could have moved, she would have, but her body felt as if it were cemented to the floor. Eden's harsh words felt like a dagger piercing into her heart. She couldn't believe it. Quinn could feel the pain and venom draining off Pandora's body.

"*Get out*," Eden bellowed, "and don't ever come near me again."

"This has gone entirely *too* far!" Quinn turned, darting her eyes at Eden.

"You know what, everybody just get out! I don't want to see anybody anymore. Just go!" Eden roared.

"Eden, you're hurting and taking all of your-"

"Get out!! Get the hell out!!!" Eden flew into a psychotic rage, nearly falling out of her bed. Andre blinked his eyes in shock, quickly bolting for the door. Quinn's heart raced while she followed, dragging Pandora with her. The second they all got out the door, three doctors ran in after them, preparing to sedate Eden. The door slammed shut, and Eden's manic screams could be heard for miles.

Quinn rubbed her temples, "this is unreal." Tears flooded the cracks of her eyes while she silently began to pray. Pandora finally regained feeling in her body, as Andre stared at her, confused.

"Pandora, what was that-" Pandora blinked her eyes, stretching her hand out to shut him up. Turning on her heels, she stormed down the hall. Andre turned, peering at his disheveled wife. "What is going *on*?"

"What's not going on?" Quinn shook her head in disbelief.

"Well, can we sit somewhere and talk about it?" He gently reached for Quinn's hand, but she drew her body back in defense.

"Keep your *filthy* hands off of me," she hissed. Andre snatched his hand back, instantly embarrassed.

"Quinn, will you please-" Quinn turned around and headed down the hallway after Pandora. She had no idea what was going on in her marriage, but she had no intentions of fixing it today. Rushing down the corridor, she stopped at the waiting room. Peering in, she looked around for Pandora, but collided with Joseph, heading out of the room. Joseph grabbed her shoulders to keep from bumping into her.

"Quinn, what's going on?" Joseph asked, concerned.

"I don't even know where to begin," she fussed, trying to keep herself from bursting into tears, "did Anna come through here?"

"Like a bat out of hell," Joseph said, "she grabbed her purse and ran down the emergency exit. What the heck—" before he could finish, Andre walked into the waiting room, stopping dead in his tracks when he saw Joseph in his wife's personal space. Glaring, his eyes immediately locked in on Joseph, clearing his throat loudly.

Joseph looked up, and Quinn jumped back, turning to face her husband.

"Hey, *Pastor,*" Joseph said sarcastically, his body growing tense, "I heard my wife had a *great* time at your church this morning."

"She had a blast." Andre scowled coldly, holding in the immediate impulse to beat the black off of Joseph.

"You know, I always told Andrea that my step-son had a familiar face. Now I know why. I can see the resemblance between you two," Joseph snarled. Quinn's heart began beating so fast, she thought it would give away.

"There is a time and a place for everything," she said, "now is not the time, and here is definat-"

"Well, with your wife being the city *slut,* I'm sure her son *does* remind you of someone in this town. It's just not me," Andre snapped back, bawling his hands into fists.

Joseph gritted his teeth as his blood boiled, hearing Andrea being called out.

"You watch your mouth talking about my wife," Joseph's nostrils flared, moving toward Andre. Quinn stepped in front of her husband. If Jesus was coming back, now would have been a good time.

"You stop writing checks with your *mouth,* that your behind can't cash," Andre bitterly spat back, moving toward Joseph.

"*Andre,*" Quinn gritted, "You are still a pastor, and you're in public," she fussed.

"Move, Quinn," Andre ordered.

"No. You guys need not-"

"Mannequin!" Andre roared like a lion. His ocean deep, masculine voice bounced off the walls. The bass from his words put the fear of God into Quinn, as she quickly jumped out of the way, obeying his demand. As Joseph moved in closer, Andre noticed lipstick on his shirt collar, the side of his neck, and the crack of his mouth. He froze in his tracks and his eyes flew open like a mad man. The deep pink that stained Joseph matched the faded pink on his wife's lips. Rage swirled up in his body like a desert storm.

"That's a familiar lipstick you're wearing, *boy,*" Andre muttered, his breathing speeding up. Quinn nearly fainted when she looked at Joseph's shirt, and face. Joseph did a double take and looked back at Andre with a smug grin. "Did you touch my wife?"

"Andre, *please*" Quinn begged in a low tone.

"I touched all-over your beautiful wife, just like you touched mine." Quinn softly shut her eyes, releasing a painful sigh. *There was getting ready to be three deaths in one day.* Andre gave Joseph a stare that would have made the devil himself, run for his life. Quinn was his pride and joy. The addiction he struggled with fueled his hunger for all the fun, enticing, bad girls who had a party on his erection, but only one woman had his heart. He would kill for Quinn's heart, and die for her love. If another man even looked at her too long, it would send him into a silent conniption. Andre's temper erupted like a volcano, as he balled his hands into a fist, punching Joseph in the face with a force that could have cracked the ground open. Quinn screamed, muffling the sound with her hands. Before she could take another breath, she felt herself being slammed against the wall, knocking the wind out of her. Andre pinned her shoulders in place, breathing heavily, as his eyes bore into hers. Quinn stared back in fright, silently praying to God that he wouldn't knock her out next. Just thinking of what Quinn and Joseph could have gotten into, angered and hurt him to the bone. His muscles convulsed, as his demented eyes transitioned into a painful stare. With a trembling chin, Andre finally let her go and stormed out of the room. Quinn gasped, clutching her chest in relief. Peering down at Joseph, she watched his body go into a full-blown seizure.

"Oh my God!" She screamed, "someone help!"

Chapter 23

One month later…

After taking a month-long hiatus from work to cleanse her mind, rationalize her thoughts, and see to it that Eden was okay, Quinn finally returned to her office. Sitting at her desk, she sifted through piles of paper, as Pandora propped herself on top of Quinn's desk, looking through her own agenda.

"So, how long was Brenner a patient of yours?" Pandora looked at her file.

"A year, maybe a year and a half," Quinn furrowed, "she came consistently, and then one day she just stopped. After I saw the news, I figured out why." Pandora perked her body posture up and faced Quinn.

"I know you'll probably think I'm crazy for asking this, but-" she paused briefly. "I'm defending her as you know, and I need to use you as an expert witness." Quinn's head shot up from her desk

"Excuse me? " Quinn replied.

"Mannequin, please?" Pandora begged.

"You're asking me to defend a criminal, are you crazy? Quinn cocked her head back, "that woman smothered her baby for no reason. I hope she goes to prison for life."

"Well, if *I* have anything to do with it, she'll be found not guilty by reason of insanity," Pandora smirked.

"Well, I pray you lose and she rots in a cell forever," Quinn shook her head in disgust, "why do you choose to represent these people?"

"Here goes the million dollar question again," Pandora chuckled, "I swear, someone has asked me that same thing, every day for the last ten years.

"I'm serious," Quinn replied, "I wouldn't be able to live with myself knowing I was responsible for allowing rapists and murderer's back into society."

"I do feel guilty at times," Pandora admitted, "but I don't allow my feelings to interfere with my money. Also, I choose to represent *these people*, because I can always find aspects in them that represent us. I love working with the accused, and the guilty. They're flawed and complicated and come to me with a sense of humility. They're a lot easier to work with. Plus, if I only represented innocent people, I'd be out of a job," Pandora laughed.

"Yes, but you're missing the point," Quinn replied, "you work *diligently* to defend them."

"I work diligently to do my job," Pandora corrected, "I *never* ask a client whether they committed the crime or not because I can't defraud the court or offer false evidence if they actually tell me they did it."

"So, you're just great liar?" Quinn rebutted.

"I don't precisely *lie*," she mischievously grinned, "I just frame my argument in terms of 'isn't it possible that someone *else* committed this crime?'" Quinn let out an annoyed breath, retreating back to her papers.

"Well, good luck with your case. I'm not helping." Pandora got up from the desk, shaking her head. "For someone to be so holy, you sure are *super* judgmental," she said, regaining Quinn's attention.

"That's not judgmental. I'm not condemning the woman to hell, I'm just choosing not to oblige."

"But Quinn," Pandora was desperate.

"Oh, Lord," Quinn sat back in her oversized chair, crossing her arms.

"A vast majority of my clients, who, for a variety of reasons, have committed crimes, but it doesn't mean they're *evil*. My baby-killing client had a baby in the midst of a nasty divorce, and she suffered from postpartum depression. She feels horrible for what she's done and regrets it. Prior to that, she was a minister at her church."

"I'm aware of all of this," Quinn sighed, "it still doesn't give her grounds to kill someone. She should have made better choices."

"Which, she *did*. She came to you for nearly two years for help, but it didn't work out for her. I feel like if she were on some type of mood altering medication, this wouldn't have happened. I mean, you said yourself she needed a psychiatric evaluation, unfortunately, it never happened because she lost her marbles." Quinn's eyes narrowed, weighing in on her statement. "Listen, she had a moment. *We all have them.* Just look at how much our lives have been affected within the past month due to moments, and quick reactions. I try to find the humanity in the people I represent, no matter what they've done. We are human, and we make mistakes. None of us would want to be defined by the worst thing we ever did." Quinn took her own actions into consideration, thinking about her own past mistakes. After a long pause to evaluate her decision, Quinn changed her mind.

"You're right. You're absolutely right...Okay, I'll help you. *This time*." Pressing her fingers to her smiling lips, Pandora playfully screamed, rushing over to Quinn, and pounced on her lap.

"I can't believe I'm agreeing to this," Quinn chuckled, shaking her head, "you are *good.*"

Pandora affectionately planted kisses on Quinn's cheeks. Thank you so much. The Judge will subpoena you and send over a court-ordered mental examination form for you to fill out. Once you fax it back, they'll get in contact with you to come in."

"My congregation is going to go into an uproar," Quinn looked worried.

"Well, they were angry with Jesus too, but look at him now!" Pandora said with excitement, "besides, who could stay mad at you with those eyes?" She winked, getting up from her friend's lap. Quinn softly smiled.

"Speaking of mad, have you talked to Andre lately?"

"No, I have not," Quinn's expression went slack, "I've been staying with Eden all month. He's called and texted, but I haven't responded," Her shoulders dropped, and her heart sank. She tried everything she could to take her mind off her husband over the last month, but it never worked for longer than a few minutes.

"Quinn, I know you're hurting, but this makes no sense," Pandora looked confused, that man loves you so much, I just don't get it."

"I use to believe that, until reality set in that he fathered another woman's child," Quinn replied flatly.

"About that," Pandora defended, "that test came back negative. David is not his son. I *knew* he wasn't." Instant chills shot down Quinn's spine,

"What?"

"They found out a couple weeks ago. You would've known, had you answered your husband's phone calls. Joe said that Andrea is supposed to be coming into your office to personally apologize," Pandora rolled her eyes, "and if I were you, when she comes in here, I would jump across my desk and *spit* in her lying face," she sneered. Quinn felt her heart freeze. She was willing to work through Andre's cheating, but having a baby by someone else just wasn't going to fly with her. Now, after finding out the accusations weren't true, Quinn felt bad for cutting off communication with him for an entire month. The look of hurt and regret was all over her face. "Anyway, Mannequin, you need to talk to your husband." Pandora nodded remorsefully.

"I will," she quickly wiped the cracks of her eyes before her tears lingered out, "when the time is right, I will."

"Okay, but please get it together soon. You two are my poster couple for marriage. If you guys don't make it, *certainly* there's no hope for me," Pandora reached into her purse for her phone. She cringed the second she glanced at her screen. "Speak of the devil, here he is texting me now."

"But you've only been married a little over thirty days," Quinn got up and walked over to her bookcase, "is it that bad already?"

"Honey, that man is driving- me- *crazy,*" Pandora massaged her temples, "I go to bed dreaming about him, and wake up cursing him out." Quinn smiled, grabbing a book from her shelf before turning to walk back to her desk.

"I think you're just being dramatic." Pandora got up from her chair and rushed over to Quinn's sofa, stretching her body on it.

"Please, *help* me," Quinn looked on, amused by Pandora's antics. "You're laughing, I'm serious," getting up from the couch, Pandora returned to her seat. "Every day we're arguing and going back and forth. This was supposed to be my happily ever after, but it's more like my nightmare on Elm street. We make love, I get over it, and then it's something else. I can't do this for the next fifty years. I'll *kill* him, bury his body in our backyard, and plant a rose garden over his dead remains."

"I believe you," Quinn laughed. "I think it's your mouth that keeps getting you into trouble. I suggest being a bit more submissive.

Pandora cringed.

"Is this how you've gotten by over the last nine years? Being a doormat?" Quinn snorted, shaking her head at her friend.

"I have never, nor will I ever, be someone's doormat," she replied, "the real strength in a woman, *especially* a headstrong woman, is not found in her ability to huff and puff, making a bunch of noise so everyone hears her. It's in her ability to stand down," Quinn pointed out. "That takes a lot of self-control and humility." Pandora listened intently.

"Think about it," Quinn got up from her chair and began to pace the floor, "I'm a psychologist, an expert on marriage and family. Do you know how challenging it is for me to yield and surrender my knowledge in different situations that take place in my marriage? I'm married to a powerful man, that leads a congregation of thousands. *Somebody's* got to step down in order for us to work, otherwise, we'd constantly be at each other's throats, arguing and bickering," Quinn scrunched her face up, "and that's not a marriage honey, that's a debate team." Pandora's eyes lowered. *She knew her ego was the reason her marriage wasn't working.*

"So, you just shut up and play the fool?" Pandora looked up again.

"Absolutely not. I know who I am, and I understand my place in this world. I'm a very powerful woman, but I use my authority here in my office, when I'm helping a patient," Quinn gestured, "or on the pulpit when I'm warring with spirits. However, when I go home, I drop my ego and position at the front door next to my shoes. My husband knows what kind of woman I am, I don't need to throw it in his face to prove anything. *That's* what submission is. Try it, I promise you your home will be a much happier place."

"I'll submit...with an attitude," Pandora rolled her eyes as Quinn shook her head and laughed, "it doesn't sound easy, but I sacrificed a lot for this marriage, so I'm willing to make it work," she sighed.

"Sacrifice is right. Have you tried reaching out to Eden, yet? Pandora's nostrils flared at the sound of Eden's name. She sprung up from her chair, causing Quinn to step out of the way.

"Thanks so much for helping me with this case," Pandora grabbed her purse, "I have to get back to my office now."

"*Joanna?*" Quinn spoke in a soft, stern voice, stepping into Pandora's personal space.

"No," Pandora responded coldly, "I have not reached out to her, and I don't plan to. I hear Miss Ruby's funeral was beautiful, and I've gone to her grave to pay my respects." Pandora knew what she did was a hard pill to swallow, but for someone who meant the world to her, to wish her dead during the most traumatic experience of her life, hurt her to her core. Pandora cried for weeks, as Eden's harsh words replayed in her mind over and over again. Finally, her heart turned to stone and she forced herself not to care or give it any more thought. Since she was dead to Eden, Eden was now dead to her.

"At some point, you two are going to have to come together and talk. This isn't some associate you've known for a few months, or a few years," Quinn's eyes bore into hers, "you guys are more than that, and it's worth more than your pride and pain. If it's not fixable, then so be it, but at *least* give it some effort."

"Are you done? I have to go," she replied in an emotionless voice. Quinn moistened her lips and stepped back.

"Fine."

Pandora high tailed it across the room and stormed out of Quinn's office. Shaking her head, Quinn walked back to her seat with a somber glow. She missed having both of her friends around and prayed every night that they could work out their differences and come back together. As she sat down at her desk, grabbing her ink pen to fill out her paperwork, her eyes glanced at a picture of her and Andre at the beach. The pain that she forced to the side, dealing with Eden and her tragedy, had all returned in an instant. Anxiety made her hands tremble, losing their grip on the ink pen she held. Quinn felt like a piece of her was missing, that she would never get back. Her day-to-day activities seemed meaningless without having someone to talk about it with when the day had ended. Eden's bed was comfortable, but she missed sleeping in her husband's strong arms. The way he looked at her, the laughter they shared, and the passionate love they made flickered through her mind like a movie. A soft knock at the door broke her out of her trance.

"Come in," she called, quickly wiping her eyes and fixing her face just as her secretary opened the door and stood in the doorway.

"Dr. Bentley, your three o'clock is here." The woman gracefully smiled. Quinn nodded back.

"Send them right in Joyce, thank you," she smiled back. Standing up to adjust her clothes, Quinn walked over to her full-size mirror.

"Just one last appointment, Quinn, hold it together for one last hour," she whispered. As her door opened, Quinn adjusted her posture, painting a welcoming smile across her face. Her heart froze and her legs nearly collapsed underneath her when Andre walked through the door.

"Good afternoon," he spoke gently, walking in and closing the door behind him. Quinn blinked rapidly before opening her stare.

"Hello," she responded, partly confused and shocked, "I-"

"Your receptionist requested that I be here fifteen minutes early to fill out paperwork, but I got stuck in traffic." He reached into his pocket, pulling out his driver's license and insurance card, "I have my information with me. You *do* take Blue Cross, correct?" He stared boldly into her eyes. Quinn's eyes dropped down to the information in his hands, before traveling back up to his face. She stared at him for a long moment, before slowly nodding her head yes.

"Great," he smiled, walking up to her. The closer he got, the more disheveled she became. "Where should I sit?" Andre asked, locking eyes on her once more. Quinn had been without him for an entire month, making it the longest they had ever gone without seeing one another. His prestige, charm, and charisma pulled at her like a magnet.

"You can sit anywhere you'd like," she responded, barely audible. Swallowing hard, she walked over to her desk and took a seat in her chair. Andre walked over to her white couch and sat down. The silence in the room was so thick, you could cut it with a knife.

"This is the first time I've ever seen a psychologist, so I'm not sure what to expect," he looked at her. "I told myself I'd never go to one because I didn't want to feel weak and powerless, as if I couldn't solve my issues on my own. But, I need help, and Google told me you were the best Psychologist in Virginia."

"How can I help you?" She spoke softly. Andre cleared his throat and rubbed a hand down his face before looking up to face his wife.

"Well, I'm a pastor, if you don't know. It wasn't a position I chose, but God's purpose for your life isn't really a choice you have the option of agreeing or disagreeing with. I spend most of my time saving souls and fixing people's problems. So much so, that I tend to forget I'm a human with problems too." Lowering his head, he fiddled with his fingers. "I have a huge problem. One that I've been able to mask, and ignore for years, but now it is spiraling out of control and ruining my life."

"When did your problem start?" Quinn asked.

"Sophmore year of college." Andre replied, that was the best *and* worst year of my life. My grades were good, my girlfriend and I made love for the first time," he grinned, "and my dad appointed me as a junior Deacon at the church. I got to be a starter for my football team, and I made a ton of friends, I couldn't have asked for anything else. I was blessed. Until –" he paused to gather his thoughts before staring his wife straight in her eyes. "One night, my coach's wife seduced me in the back of a bus." Quinn's eyes squinted, as her mouth began to open. "I, I asked her to stop, but she was persistent. She touched all over me until I started to like it. Eventually, we ended up sleeping together, and she introduced me to the world of vulgarity and perversion," Andre shook his head, wiping the sweat from his brow. "I laid down with that woman and got up with her demons. Her strongholds got a hold of me, and I was never able to look at sex the same," his eyebrows gathered into a pained stare. The look of disgust was written all over him. "My mind became excessively preoccupied with it, twenty four hours a day. I would make mad, passionate love to my girlfriend, and then masturbate to dirty images, and obscene thoughts. I'd be in church, secretly watching porn from my phone while my dad preached. I was never a fan of loose women, either. Girls who walked around practically nude, were a huge turnoff for me. I loved the fact that my girlfriend was a lady in public, and that I was the only man to ever see her cleavage," Tears welled up in Andre's eyes as he bit his lip, nervously tapping his leg up and down, "but, all of a sudden, I found myself sneaking into strip clubs. I was having sex with strippers, hookers, whores, everything that was dirty and disgusting, I did it, and I couldn't stop," tears rushed down his face. "It got so bad and out of control at one point, I tried to commit suicide.

My mind was so consumed and wrapped up in perversion, I grabbed my dad's power drill, and put it to my temple in an attempt to drill the thoughts out of my head." Using her elbow for support, Quinn used her hand to support her mouth as her wide, tear-filled eyes watched her husband from afar. "The drill was fully charged, but it didn't work for some reason. I begged and pleaded with God to fix me, and shortly after that, I took over my dad's church. I saw that as God answering my prayers. I buried my demons, got married, and stayed faithful to my wife. For years, the women would taunt, and tease me from the pulpit. I fought it, and fought it, and fought some more, until seven months ago when it got to be too much. Dirty thoughts started corrupting my mind and I felt so guilty, I couldn't look my wife in her eyes anymore. Her love was so innocent, and pure, and I felt like I didn't deserve it. My past started to haunt me, and the guilt and shame from it all forced me to avoid her. The more distant we became, the stronger my urges became, until I finally folded and slept with a woman in my congregation. I wouldn't be the man I am today if it weren't for my wife, and to know how much my issues have affected her, eats me alive. I have been crazy in love with her since the first time I laid eyes on her. She's like my kryptonite; I'm powerless without her. If she ever left me, I would probably die from a broken heart." He paused for a long moment, boring into Quinn's eyes. "*I need help.*" Andre sat on Quinn's sofa, nearly drowning in his tears. He had so much more to say, but the damage he had done, and the guilt he felt, drained what little energy he had left. The tormenting images of Quinn's lipstick prints all over another man, gave him nightmares every time he fell asleep.

A little piece of him died every day he woke up without her in his arms. Andre was a wreck. He lowered his head into his forearms and wished he could have disappeared. He felt like a failure, and the things he had done seemed unforgivable. He felt like a crooked pastor and a disappointment to his late parents. They left him thousands of souls to tend after, and he let them down. He silently prayed to himself, asking God for mercy. Before he got to "amen," he felt a soft, angelic touch, caress his shoulder. Andre lifted his head to see Quinn squat down in front of him, her own tears trickling down her face. Her eyes were filled with a bittersweet mixture of pain, hurt, compassion, and unconditional love. She slowly stood up, pulling him up with her. Quinn wrapped her arms around his neck, pressing herself against him. He wrapped his arms around her waist, welcoming her embrace. She'd just found out a few days ago that she was three months pregnant. She didn't know anything about the prenatal stages of development, or how big the baby was, but she wondered if he could feel it moving. The instant they connected, they both felt possessed. They were lost, drowning in the powerful joy of being held by one another. Thirty days spent alone, taught them how miserable, dull, and colorless their world was without each other in it. Their touch was so powerful to one another, no more words were needed. In due time, everything felt like it would be all right. To the world, Mannequin and Andre were a spitting image of perfection. Society thought they were given the gift of marital bliss, and everybody wanted it. Little did they know, the gift box was filled with illusions, and tied with bows of wishful thinking. Their love was anything but blissful. Behind closed doors, when the masks of false romanticism had fallen off, they were just two flawed human beings. Sometimes they failed each other, and many times their love fell short. But in failures and shortcomings they never tapped out or gave up. Like Romeo and Juliette, they too were a beautifully written tragedy that persevered in love's name. Their marriage was so far from what the adversary had planned and written for their ending. But as though many of his weapons were formed, they would never prosper here. Love wins; *every time.*

Chapter 24

Eden laid in a lifeless, fetal position in her mother's queen sized bed, clutching her pillow. It was the first time she had been alone since Ruby's death. Over the last month, Eden had Quinn by her side. Quinn put the world on pause to see to it that Eden was okay. Quinn set up Ruby's funeral arrangements, picked out her casket, and secured her final resting place at the graveyard. She took a vacation from work and stayed by Eden's side from sun up to sun down. She cooked, cleaned up, and grocery shopped for Eden. She was there to talk, listen, and sit around doing nothing. At night, Quinn cuddled next to her, and held on tight while Eden begged God for her mother back, and cried herself to sleep. Quinn even showered with her, because Eden couldn't stomach being alone. There was nothing her best friend wouldn't do for her, and she was beyond grateful. However, Quinn was a busy woman with a husband and a host of important responsibilities. Eden knew the day would come when she would have to leave, and here it was. Ruby's home was deathly quiet, but the thoughts in Eden's mind were noisy as ever. She had spent the last few days preoccupying herself with chores and loud music, anything to keep her mind off her mother, and her daughter. She didn't want to grieve anymore, but grief didn't run on her schedule, it had an agenda of its own. Eden took in the scent of Ruby's perfume in her bed sheets, and for a split second, it felt like she was close by. Reaching into her pocket for her cell-phone, Eden dialed her mother's number and hoped she would answer, and she didn't, but she knew that already. A man's voice answered instead, and Eden hung up. Tears filled her eyes and her chest felt like it was beginning to cave in. Ruby's phone number had already been transferred, and her name had been re-placed. Eden sat straight up, rocking herself back and forth. Her world was stretched beyond repair and she wrestled within it, trying to find a space to survive in her head. Ruby was her first friend. She rocked her as a baby, patched her up as a clumsy kid, and eased her heartache as a teenager. When Eden graduated college and chased around a boy instead of her mas-ter's degree, her mother was disappointed, but still supported her. She coached her on the ins and outs of being a first-time mother and walked her through all the changes that happened with her pregnant body. Ruby owned several businesses and always saw to it that her only child was well taken care of. Even in death, she'd left her a fortune, but Eden didn't care about the money. She had her spoiled moments, but she was never a rotten child. Eden loved her moth-er more than anything in the world. Her best friends did too. Quinn lost her mother after high school, and Pandora grew distant from hers after she was kid-napped. Ruby mothered and cared for both of them in the same way she did Eden. She helped Quinn plan her wedding and funded Pandora's college education. Tears began rushing down Eden's face, as she stood up and began walking through her mother's empty home. The reality that she would never see her again began to settle. She was born from her mother, and her body acutely felt the physical loss of her. She would never feel the warmth of her hand or hear the sound of her laugh. Eden could no longer ask about her family history, medical questions, or how to do life, questions. Eden's life was just beginning, and there was so much her mother would miss. As she reached the hallway, her legs began to tremble and her mind grew delirious. She slammed herself against the wall and slid her body to the floor, screaming in agony.

Downstairs...

Pandora walked into Ruby's complex. The second her foot stepped into the building, she felt her legs growing weak and her stomach growing tight. Ruby purchased her condo two weeks after Quinn and Pandora's senior prom. Pandora remembered hearing Ruby scream with the biggest smile plastered across her face, watching her and Quinn race into the lobby to see it. Pandora walked through the entrance and proceeded into the lobby. Immediately, she remembered the day she ran away from home. She stepped into Ruby's lobby with two big plastic bags, and a face full of tears. Ruby laughed obnoxiously at Pandora's homeless appearance, and then gripped her up into the warmest hug, welcoming her into her home. If it weren't for Ruby keeping her out of trouble and making sure she went to college, Pandora would have never amounted to the powerful, privileged woman she was today. She owed Ruby her whole life, and she was crushed to the bone that she couldn't even go to her funeral to say goodbye. Pandora bit her bottom lip, blinking her eyes to resist the urge to scream, as she stepped into the elevator and pressed the button to Ruby's floor.

"Why did I come here?" Pandora asked out loud, quickly wiping the tears that forced themselves from her eyelids. Quinn's words to Pandora after leaving her office pierced her heart to the point where she put her pride aside and came to Eden's house to try and reconcile. She missed her friend so much and wanted so badly to be there for her. The world saw Pandora as ruthless, and cold hearted, and Pandora could've cared less. Being disliked and hated came with her job, but having either of her friend's think of her as the devil, tore her ego to pieces. As the elevator traveled up to the tenth floor, Pandora could still feel the fire from the passionate lust her and Jackson left in it. She lowered her head, trying aimlessly to think of something else as guilt began to creep up on her. Pandora fixed her flustered demeanor when the elevator door opened. She stepped off, proceeding down the hallway to Ruby's door. Pandora loved Jackson so much, but she felt like half a person without her best friend. She missed Eden's humble smile and bright eyes. She missed seeing her waddle and hearing her complain about the unwanted symptoms pregnancy brought. Pandora couldn't stand kids, but she couldn't wait to hold and spoil Eden's daughter. As a lawyer, she knew that one impulsive decision could change your life in an instant, but she never imagined it would happen to her. As she reached Ruby's door, she took out her keys. Knowing Eden probably wouldn't let her in, she took it upon herself to invite herself in. Pandora unlocked the door and took a deep breath, slowly entering the condo. Her thoughts raced and her heart began to accelerate as she thought of Eden's episode in the hospital. Her heart couldn't take seeing her in that much pain again, and she hoped to God Eden was doing much better. The whole house seemed dreary and empty as Pandora closed the door, and laid her purse and keys on the dining room table. She crossed her arms and slowly made her way into the living room.

"Ede-" Before Eden's name could finish escaping her lips, she spotted her by the closet door, hanging from her neck by a thick rope, attached to something on the ceiling. Eden's face was a nasty shade of purple, and her mouth had foam coming from it. Her legs twitched horribly. Pandora momentarily froze like a monument, as fear clutched her heart, her throat, and her legs.

"Jesus Christ!" She yelled in a shrill, pained voice, as her arms began to shake. Pandora rushed into the kitchen and grabbed a sharp knife from the drawer. She ran over to Eden and stood on the chair beside her dangling body. Pandora could barely breathe as her body trembled in fear. Using all of her strength, she cut the rope, causing Eden to plunge into the floor. Immediately, Eden manically gasped for air, holding her neck with terrified, widened eyes. Pandora could feel her pulse through her ears as she dropped to the floor and propped Eden's body up. "Eden, take your time. Breath slower, more controlled," Pandora coached in a panic, tears streaming down her face like a faucet. Pandora untied the rope from her neck as Eden gasped for each breath like it were her last, until finally regaining control. "Oh my God," Pandora cried, shaking. "Can you breathe okay?" Eden coughed, slowly nodding her head while she continued to get herself together. Pandora aggressively used her hands to turn Eden's head in her direction. "Please don't do *anything* like this, again!" She screamed, desperately, "there is no way in hell I'd be able to live like a sane human being if something happened to you." Finally catching her breath, Eden's own tears began to form and she began to cry. She wanted to die so badly and wished Pandora wouldn't have stopped her.

"Why are you in my house? Get out," Eden whispered through her tears.

"No," Pandora replied sternly, "I'm not going anywhere. You need me, and I'm staying right here." Eden forcefully got up from the floor, as Pandora followed.

"Pandora, leave me alone, I hate you. Get out!" She screamed until she was red in the face. Pandora moved into her, wrapping her arms around Eden, while Eden forcefully tried to push her off. "Get *off* of me, I hate you!" She shrieked, but Pandora closed her eyes, refusing to let go. Eden wiggled and screamed until her struggle weakened and her scream turned into a heart-breaking sob. "Please, let me go," she begged, "get out, and let me die," her body lost its balance and leaned on Pandora. Pandora slowly lowered herself to the floor, bringing Eden with her. Rubbing Eden's back, she silently cried with her.

"I'm so sorry to see you suffer like this," Pandora shook her head, "but you have your whole life ahead of you, and friends who love you to death. Don't do anything stupid like this again," She fussed.

"You don't love me," Eden cried, "friends don't stab each other in the back the way you did." Using her free hand to wipe her tears, Pandora let go of Eden and looked her directly in her face.

"Eden, listen to me okay? You only get one life. I spent most of mine in a shell, hiding from myself. My world is so complicated. Nothing ever made sense, until I fell in love. Time and choices, that's all we get. I left Jackson alone for the sake of our friendship, but my heart kept pulling and tugging at me until I gave it what it desired," she sniffed, shaking her head, "I'm not sorry that I married him, I love him. I *am* sorry that putting myself first took a toll on our friendship. I meant to look out for *me*, but I didn't mean to hurt *you*. I love you." Tears continued to flow from Eden's face as her lips curled. The one thing she could always expect from Pandora was the unapologetic truth. She knew how much Pandora and Jackson loved each other, and she wanted her friend to be happy, just not at the expense of her own heart. Pandora had done everything for her, growing up. She put Eden's needs before her own more times than she could have imagined, so Eden quickly understood Pandora's selfishness to herself for once. In a short period of time, Eden had lost everything that meant something to her, including Pandora. Ruby was never coming back, and neither was her newborn daughter. Pandora had returned, however, and even though Eden was suffering from her reality, she wanted her friend back. The warm embrace she extended, let Pandora know it.

"I love you too," Eden responded faintly. Pandora neglected her falling tears to gently wipe away Eden's.

"*Promise* me you'll never do anything like this again?" Pandora pleaded as Eden lowered her head.

"I feel so alone," she proclaimed, "I miss my mom so much, and there's nothing I can do about it."

"I know you miss her," Pandora responded placing Eden's hands into her own, "we all do. But Ruby didn't leave you because she wanted to, she left because there were other plans for her. She was greater than this world, and now it's up to you to live on in her memory." Eden nodded as more tears filled her eyes.

"I know, I just can't seem to accept it. It hurts so bad that I try to keep my mind off of it. I do everything possible to avoid thinking about her, and suddenly, I felt like I couldn't take it anymore"

"Baby girl, if you don't deal with grief, grief will deal with you," Pandora continued to wipe away the onset of Eden's tears, "you can try to preoccupy your mind and stay busy all you want, it *will* catch up to you. Remember that time Ruby's twin sister died?"

"Yeah, I'll never forget that, they were so close," Eden nodded.

"Exactly, and your mom told us the news as if she were having a general conversation. She stayed strong and kept it moving, like it didn't even affect her. And then two months later, she lost her other sister and reacted the same way, unaffected, like she was superhuman."

Eden nodded as she reminisced.

"That's her. Always trying to be superwoman."

"Then, six months later, remember when we were all sitting in the living room, and the neighbor knocked on the door to say her cat had died?" Pandora pressed her lips together and closed her eyes to keep herself from laughing.

"Yeah," Eden chuckled, shaking her head. "And then she freaked out."

"She had a fit! Throwing stuff, kicking, screaming, rocking back and forth," Pandora replied with an unforced laugh, as Eden giggled. "Please, deal with your issues as they happen. Don't be like *her* and wait until we're out shopping or something, and the store doesn't have your size, and you go into a conniption."

Eden burst into laughter, as Pandora joined in. They both sat on the floor reminiscing and laughing until subconsciously, Pandora taught Eden how to breathe again. There was an unexplainable underground connection in Pandora that showed up when Eden needed it most. Friendship is one of the most beautiful, powerful, and most valuable treasures in your life. *Friends hold our history.* They remember, and they bring you back home to who you are.

To be continued....

Made in the USA
Lexington, KY
04 December 2019